Also by Martha Freeman

The Secret Cookie Club

Campfire Cookies

Effie Starr Zook Has One More Question

Zap!

MARTHA FREEMAN

THE
SECRET COOKIE CLUB
P.S. SEND MORE
COOKIES

A Paula Wiseman Book
Simon & Schuster Books for Young Readers
New York   London   Toronto   Sydney   New Delhi

SIMON & SCHUSTER BOOKS FOR YOUNG READERS

An imprint of Simon & Schuster Children's Publishing Division

1230 Avenue of the Americas, New York, New York 10020

This book is a work of fiction. Any references to historical events, real people, or real places are used
fictitiously. Other names, characters, places, and events are products of the author's imagination, and any
resemblance to actual events or places or persons, living or dead, is entirely coincidental.

Text copyright © 2017 by Martha Freeman

Cover and chapter opener illustrations copyright © 2017 by Brenna Vaughn

SIMON & SCHUSTER BOOKS FOR YOUNG READERS is a trademark of Simon & Schuster, Inc.

For information about special discounts for bulk purchases, please contact Simon & Schuster Special
Sales at 1-866-506-1949 or business@simonandschuster.com.

The Simon & Schuster Speakers Bureau can bring authors to your live event.
For more information or to book an event, contact the Simon & Schuster Speakers Bureau
at 1-866-248-3049 or visit our website at www.simonspeakers.com.

Also available in a Simon & Schuster Books for Young Readers hardcover edition

Book design by Krista Vossen

The text for this book was set in Kepler Std.

Manufactured in the United States of America

0418 OFF

First Simon & Schuster Books for Young Readers paperback edition May 2018

2 4 6 8 10 9 7 5 3 1

The Library of Congress has cataloged the hardcover edition as follows:

Names: Freeman, Martha, 1956- author.

Title: P.S. send more cookies / Martha Freeman.

Description: First edition. | New York : Simon & Schuster Books for Young Readers, [2017]. | Series: The
Secret Cookie Club | "A Paula Wiseman Book." | Summary: After the girls of Flowerpot Cabin leave summer
camp, they face challenges as Grace is volunteered to dogsit, Emma faces loss, Olivia's brother starts a
family feud, and Lucy's father comes back into her life. Includes cookie recipes.

Identifiers: LCCN 2016048461| ISBN 9781481448246 (hardback) | ISBN 9781481448253 (pbk) | ISBN
9781481448260 (ebook)

Subjects: | CYAC: Friendship—Fiction. | Schools—Fiction. | Family life—Fiction. | Cookies—Fiction. |
Clubs—Fiction. | BISAC: JUVENILE FICTION / Family / General (see also headings under Social Issues). |
JUVENILE FICTION / Social Issues / Friendship. | JUVENILE FICTION / Girls & Women.

Classification: LCC PZ7.F87496 Ps 2017 | DDC [Fic]—dc23

LC record available at https://lccn.loc.gov/2016048461

For my cousin, Nancy Blossom, who shepherded
me through my first summer camp experience.

P.S. SEND MORE
COOKIES

Jack broke Hannah's heart on a Friday afternoon, which pretty much guaranteed Hannah a rotten weekend. She knew what all the bloggers she followed would say: Go out! See your besties! Indulge in a little retail therapy!

Do not, *do not* stay in, wallowing in self-pity!

What did she do? Stayed in, wallowing in self-pity.

Also, homework. Hannah was a sophomore in college. She had decided to study art history because ever

MARTHA FREEMAN

since she first saw them as a little kid she had thought Impressionist paintings were the prettiest things in the world. But now, after a year of classes, she was learning to like the sculptures the Greeks had carved out of marble. Some of them were more than two thousand years old. Over the centuries, they had lost legs and arms and chunks of their faces, but you could still see classical perfection shining through.

Not like Jack, Hannah thought.

He was overweight. He was loud. He wore this weird old-man-style hat all the time.

So why was she lying on her bed in her dorm room on a perfectly nice fall Sunday staring at her textbook and reaching for yet another tissue to wipe her tears?

Hannah decided to make some cookies. Her grandfather had been a baker who believed cake, cookies, and cupcakes had the power to fix most problems—*flour power*, he called it.

True, the bloggers she followed would be horrified. They were anti-gluten, anti-sugar, anti-fat. They lived on kale smoothies, seaweed, and chia seeds.

And they should all just settle down, Hannah thought.

Sure, an all-cookie all-the-time diet would be a recipe for disaster. But a few cookies now and then are exactly what sanity demands.

On the second floor of the dorm was a kitchen kept decently stocked with sugar, flour, and other basics. Hannah stuffed a wad of tissues in the pocket of her jeans, got up, stretched, and headed out her door and down the hall, which was deserted. Only the lovelorn would be indoors on such a beautiful day.

Hannah had met Jack at the Moonlight Ranch Summer Camp in Arizona, where they were both counselors. For a long time, they were friendly, but no sparks flew. Then one day she realized that not only was he funny, he was also someone who listened to what you said and remembered it later.

Besides, who cared that his abs weren't washboard when his eyes were so beautiful?

Jack and Hannah had gotten together about two weeks before the end of camp.

In the kitchen, she counted on her fingers. That was

six weeks ago. She was crying over a romance that had lasted a measly six weeks!

Get a grip, she told herself at the same time her phone *bee-bee-beep*ed like the Roadrunner. She had a text from Jack.

CHAPTER TWO

Tuesday, September 19, Grace

The day I found the package addressed to me in our mailbox I had a lot on my mind. Besides the usual stuff, there was an extra thing that was extra worrying. My best friend, Shoshi Rubinstein, had asked me to walk King, her family's big furry collie dog, when they went to New Hampshire for her cousin's wedding.

If I ever have a dog, it will be a small dog, not a big one like King who thinks it's fun to jump up and put his paws on the shoulders of innocent seventh-grade girls such as me and then knock the girls over and lick their faces.

I think it's fun *not* to be knocked over and *not* to have my face licked.

Therefore, big dogs and I are incompatible.

Usually Shoshi's family would send King to a pet resort, but Shoshi's brother is in college now, and they have to save money. So Shoshi thought of me. All I have to do is clip the leash to King's collar and walk him around the block twice and (yuck!*)* clean up after him.

"It's super easy," she told me. This was at lunch the same day I found the package. Shoshi and I were sitting with Nell and Deirdre at our usual table. "King loves his walk. He'll be glad to see you. My parents will pay you. Anything's cheaper than the pet resort."

"They don't have to pay me," I said.

"Oh, that's really nice, Grace. Thanks," Shoshi said. "I can give you a key at school on Friday, okay? The wedding's on Saturday, and we'll be back Sunday afternoon. You just have to walk him Friday night, twice on Saturday and once Sunday morning."

"Uh . . . ," I said, because I hadn't exactly meant to agree. I had just meant that I did not want money.

"Uh, what?" Shoshi raised her eyebrows and took a big bite of tuna sandwich.

I looked hopefully at Deirdre and Nell, but neither of them said a word. Anyway, they don't live as close to Shoshi's house as I do.

"Uh, nothing," I said. "Okay." It was already too late to back out. If I did, I would be a terrible friend.

So anyway, later that same afternoon, I grabbed the mail out of the mailbox at the end of our driveway as usual, saw the package, and read the return address: Hannah Lehrer, Floral Park, NY.

Here is the embarrassing part. With so much on my mind, it took me about two seconds to remember who Hannah Lehrer was. Then I did remember and then I squealed (also embarrassing). Hannah Lehrer was good old Hannah, my counselor at Moonlight Ranch!

I was glad to hear from her, but the best part was this: There must be cookies in that package!

After our first summer at Moonlight Ranch, the four Flowerpot campers—Emma, Olivia, Lucy, and I—formed the Secret Cookie Club. The idea was to take turns sending homemade cookies to each other so we'd stay in touch through the school year.

As the name says, it was supposed to be a secret, but Hannah found out, and at the end of camp this summer, she said she wanted to join too. We could not exactly turn her down. The idea of cookies having the power fix things had come from her—or more accurately, from her grandfather the baker. She had even given each of us some of his recipes.

Now I could hardly wait to open that box. Cookies from Hannah would be delicious, and her timing was perfect. After two hours of ballet, I was starving, and my parents would not be home from work to nuke dinner for another hour at least.

I unlocked the front door, threw the rest of my

family's mail on the counter, took out a kitchen knife, and tore the package open. Instantly, I was over-whelmed by a wonderful combination of smells—lemon, sugar, and butter.

Before I even noticed that Hannah had enclosed a letter, too, I had drunk half a glass of milk and eaten two of the perfectly round, white-frosted lemon cookies.

I had a lot of homework, but even so I decided I could spare a few minutes to sit in the plaid recliner in the family room and read Hannah's letter.

Sunday, Sept. 17

Dear Grace,

I am not sure if my membership application for the Secret Cookie Club thas been approved, but I baked an extra-big batch today, and I didn't think you'd mind if I mailed you some.

This is one of my grandpa's recipes but not one I gave you

guys last summer, I don't think. Some people don't like lemon that much. I know you will, though, because you are more sophisticated than the average seventh grader.

Everything is totally fine with me, especially school, which is very interesting. I am taking a class about old paintings on the walls of caves. Some of the pictures are horses, which makes me nostalgic for Moonlight Ranch and my four campers, too.

I am even a little bit nostalgic for Lance. Do you remember him? The cute counselor from Silver Spur Cabin? For a while I thought you four were trying to fix him and me up. It's probably too bad that didn't work because Jack (the counselor from Yucca Cabin—you probably remember him because he wears a stupid hat all the time) texted me Friday to say he thought we should "see other people."

How unoriginal is that!

And then (I might as well tell you the whole story) he

texted me Sunday that the Friday text had been a big mistake and would I PLEASE forgive him? (Crying face, crying face, crying face, broken heart, roses.)

Of course my answer to that was not till the sun burns out! (Dagger, dagger, dagger, H-bomb.)

Who does he think he is anyway? As Olivia would say, Jack is not worth the nail on my pinky toe.

So sorry, Grace, if that was TMI. But it's good if you learn now what some men are like so you can avoid trouble later.

Not that there's any trouble for me anymore. Like I said, everything is totally fine. My grandpa was right about flour power!

Please say hello to your parents for me. And save them a cookie or two. (Ha-ha!)

Love,

Your one and only Flowerpot Cabin counselor, Hannah

P.S. I didn't have enough cookies to send boxes to all four of my campers. So if you're in touch with Emma, Olivia, and Lucy, tell them they will get their cookies later!

CHAPTER THREE

Grace

I am ashamed to say that I did not jump up and tackle homework the moment I finished reading Hannah's letter the way I'd planned to.

Instead, I read the letter again. And the second time a million questions flooded my brain. How could Jack have been so stupid? Was Hannah really okay like she said she was? And how had she figured out we were trying to fix her up with Lance?

We had been very, very sneaky!

It was too bad that of all us Secret Cookie Club members, I was totally the least qualified to advise Hannah on romance. Olivia knows all about boys. She has a new one every week. Emma is understanding and wise about every kind of problem. Lucy knows a lot because she has a front-row seat on her divorced mom's soap-opera life.

Then there is me, Grace. I had a boyfriend once. His name was Vivek. It lasted four days. End of story.

Should I call Emma or Olivia? Text them? If you can believe it, Lucy does not have a phone of her own, and besides her mom (who is never home), she lives with her grandmother, and even *she* thinks her grandmother is scary.

I decided not to call anybody—at least not yet. It was possible Hannah did not actually want our help with her love life. The help we gave her last summer had not worked out the way we thought. Besides, didn't I have enough responsibilities in my life—including now a new one, Shoshi's stupid dog, King?

I hoped I was not being selfish, but for now Hannah

would have to look elsewhere for wise advice about boys.

When my parents got home—dad first, as usual—they said hello, went upstairs to change, came back down, and started fixing dinner. They are both engineers. They are both efficient.

My parents are Joe Xi and Anna Burrowes. Dad is Chinese, born in Singapore. Mom was born in Germany, but her family is from New England. Her dad worked for the US government, so she was raised all over the world.

Most people when they meet me assume I am Chinese through and through, but in the mirror I see a little of each of my parents—my mom's pointy nose, my dad's round face.

One good thing about eating dinner from the freezer is you get to have whatever you want. That night I picked pot stickers, and my parents shared a pizza. For health, we shared a big bowl of snap peas. As usual, we sat at the kitchen counter. This was Wednesday, and the housecleaners don't come till Friday. We shoved newspapers and catalogs out of the way to make places for ourselves.

Both my parents have long commutes from where they work near Boston to our house in Groton. A lot of the time they come home cranky. That day was the same until I told them about the cookies.

"Excellent news," my father said.

"I love lemon," my mother said.

"Are there plenty?" my father asked. "Where are they?"

"I put them away for dessert," I said. "You have to be patient."

My parents remembered that Hannah was my counselor and about the cookies last year too.

"It's a charming tradition you girls have started," my mother said. "How is Hannah doing in college?"

"Fine," I said, thinking Hannah might not want me blabbing about her boy troubles. "She is taking a class about paintings in caves."

My mother frowned. "Not practical," she said.

"Must everything be practical?" my father asked.

"Hmmm," said my mother, which was her way of saying yes without arguing.

"Is piano practical?" I asked. "Is ballet?" I was feeling a little like Snot-Nosed Grace—the rude girl that lurks beneath the surface of my nice, polite self. For a long time my parents did not know Snot-Nosed Grace existed, but lately she has been speaking up more often.

"Piano and ballet teach discipline, physical fitness, and coordination," said my mother. "So of course they're practical. Aren't they, Joe?"

"Hmmm," said my father.

After that, my parents asked the usual questions about homework and activities. I gave the usual answers, but I was really thinking about King. Eventually, I had to tell my parents about him. He was going to stay at his own house, but I would still need their permission to go over and take care of him. Sometimes it's annoying to have parents. They are always paying attention. Sometimes I wish I were grown up and no one knew what I did or cared.

I waited till both my parents were chewing. Then I told them I had agreed to watch the Rubinsteins' dog.

My mother swallowed her food in a lump. "That big dog?"

"I thought you had a project due on Monday," said my father.

In case it's not obvious, my family does not have pets. Neither of my parents grew up with them, and neither sees the point of additional responsibility. According to them, the modern family's schedule does not include time for anything other than work, house, and children—or in their case, work, house, and child.

"He's not dangerous, and I'll still have time for homework," I said. "But I am a little nervous. I never walked a dog before, never picked up his poop. I'm not sure I'll be good at it."

"Certain things should not be mentioned during dinner," said my mother.

"I'm sure you'll do very well," said my father.

"I think you should reconsider," said my mother. "He's a big dog, and you're a small girl. The Rubinsteins still have time to find someone else, someone more experienced."

I thought I should reconsider too, but when my mom said it, I got stubborn. "I am not that small. It will be fine. It's you who doesn't like dogs."

Now, my mother—who always claims to be a feminist—appealed to my father. "Tell her she isn't allowed to, Joe. Tell her."

My father looked thoughtful and dabbed his lips with a paper napkin. "I think," he said at last, "that Grace is old enough to make the decision for herself."

CHAPTER FOUR

Grace

After chess club the next afternoon, I went over to Shoshi's to see the dog equipment and give King a trial walk.

If you ask me, King has a mental disorder—a split personality perhaps. When I was outside on the porch, he barked and growled as if I were a space invader. When I was inside in the hall, he acted like I was his favorite long-lost friend. His tail wagged like an eggbeater. His tongue could not lick my face fast enough.

"He's giving you doggy kisses, Grace!" said Shoshi.

Did she think this was a good thing?

On the trial walk, I learned that King does not behave like the dogs in the show ring on TV. Instead he zigzags so that the leash slithers on the sidewalk like a snake. But for all the ballet, I would have tripped. Shoshi told me I was catching on fast.

"You'll be okay with him, right, Grace?" she said in the hall when I was getting ready to leave.

I said, "Sure," because I was sure it was what she wanted to hear.

"Great." Shoshi grinned. "Because King is really a lovable goofball, but he can seem kind of intimidating, plus he's big and you're not. But you're good at everything, right? So that means dog walking, too."

"I am probably not good at everything," I said.

"Name one thing you're not good at," Shoshi said.

"You are a better artist than me," I said.

"But you're still good at art, right?" Shoshi said.

I admitted that I am. Then I thought of something. "I

have never tried fishing. Maybe I'm not good at that. I don't think I would like fish guts."

"That's like the poop part of dog walking," Shoshi said. "But not liking it doesn't make you bad. Just pay attention so King doesn't eat what he shouldn't, and hold on tight to his leash."

It is four blocks from Shoshi's house to my house. Up until last year, my parents would not have let me walk so far by myself. They would have told me to wait till they could pick me up in the car. But since Shoshi and I got to be friends, I have been allowed to do more things. With an older brother and an older sister, Shoshi has more freedom than I do. When my parents saw she had survived, they gave me more freedom too.

I checked the mailbox as usual when I got home, and guess what? There was a letter for me—two things in two days! A minor miracle!

Even before I looked at the return address, I knew the letter was from Lucy, my camp friend who lives in Beverly Hills. She is the only person I know who writes real, paper-and-ink letters.

There were a few of Hannah's lemon cookies left, so for the second day in a row I put off homework to eat cookies and read a letter.

Saturday, Sept. 16

Hi Grace!

How are you? (And don't say "busy" because I already know. I bet you have five after-school activities and one hundred hours of homework every night!)

Have you gotten over Vivek yet? And no, before you ask, he hasn't written to me or anything, which is sad but only because I was hoping for pictures of his new baby brother/sister. (I can't remember which, can you?) I bet the new baby is cute, whatever it is, and I wonder what they named it, and that is probably more than enough about Vivek.

I guess I am baby-obsessed because Kendall, the mom of the triplets I watch after school, is pregnant! My nana immediately said, "How many kids are in there this time?" which my mom said was "crude and tactless," but then my mom wanted to know too, and this time the answer is only one, a girl, that is due soon, and they are naming her Piper.

If I ever have a baby, I am going to name her either Jane or Mary.

Speaking of Arlo, Mia, and Levi (the triplets—now age four), they were super good right after I got home from Santa Barbara, where I went after camp to stay with my Aunt Freda, because they (the triplets) really missed me, Kendall said, but now they are back to being their normal bad selves. Even so, I love them a bunch, and I think I would be bored and sad if I didn't get to watch them.

Change of topic: For two days, my family actually owned a computer. It was Officer Leonard's old one. (Officer Leonard is my mom's boyfriend. You might remember he gave my mom and me a ride on the first day of camp.) I was excited about communicating with my fellow humans on Planet Earth, but then the computer died. Its death is still a mystery, but Officer Leonard said he will investigate.

My mom and I call this The Case of the Computer's Untimely Demise.

Officer Leonard and my mom have been together for more than three months, which is approaching a record for my mom. Having a cop around has been weird but also sort of good. Here is something I have learned: Most people who lie to the police are bad at it, and the police hear the same lies over and over.

Moral of the story: Do not lie to the police.

In school I still like art, and I still have Mrs. Coatrak and she still thinks I'm great, so it's nice that somebody does besides Aunt Freda, and Arlo, Mia, and Levi.

Oh, and here is some other news. My father has resurfaced. He is staying with my aunt Freda in Santa Barbara and says he wants to come for a visit. Stay tuned.

Now write to me and tell me what is going on in your life, and if there is a problem (I hope not!), I will send cookies to fix it, and if there is not a problem (I hope so!), then I will just send cookies.

So either way: cookies!

Love ya lots

—Lucy

P.S. If you are still friends with Vivek
on Facebook, would you mind telling me
what you know about the baby?

When I finished Lucy's letter and laid it in my lap my
emotions were all helter-skelter. I didn't read it again. I
took a deep breath, folded it neatly, and returned it to
the envelope.

The letter hadn't said much about camp, but still it
brought back camp memories. I imagined riding my
horse, Katinka, in the hot Arizona sun, settling into my
narrow bunk with the thin mattress at night, listening
to the clear, loud sound of the bell that woke us every
morning.

Now that summer was over, camp felt like a
stretched-out perfect time without one problem. I
knew in my head that this was not accurate. In fact,

the summer had included drama, annoyance, and even (for a few minutes) fear. But in my heart that was nothing compared with what was good.

Also, what could possibly be more scary or annoying than taking care of a too-furry pony-size dog?

So that was one feeling. But another feeling was annoyance. Because, seriously, Lucy? Did you really have to bring up Vivek?

What did I care about some new baby? (I knew it was a sister. I had never unfriended him on Facebook.)

What did I care about Vivek at all?

I wondered if Lucy knew that a long time ago I used to worry that Vivek liked her better than me. Probably she didn't know. It would have been mean to bring him up at all if she did, and Lucy isn't mean.

In fact, that was the third feeling. The letter reminded me how I really missed her and wished she were here. Since her family situation is unusual, she is more used to being on her own than most kids I know. Lucy would never be freaked out by taking care of a dog, even a dog as big as King.

All afternoon I had been wishing my dad had forbidden me taking care of him. Then I could have gone to Shoshi to say so, and I would have been off the hook, and it wouldn't have been my fault.

But my dad had said the decision was mine. And so I was really stuck.

CHAPTER FIVE

Grace

All day Friday, my stomach worried about King. I hardly even ate lunch. After school, my mom was picking me up, so Shoshi and I walked down the corridor and out the school doors together.

"Do you have any last-minute questions?" Shoshi asked. "I hope we didn't forget anything."

"I hope so too," I said.

"Anyway, my mom left you a note with phone

numbers. So if you need anything, you can call," she said. "Even though we're going to be kind of out in the woods, I think there will be cell reception."

"Wait—there might *not* be?" I said.

By this time, we had made our way down the hall and out the door and to the curb in the school parking lot where the parents wait for kids. Shoshi's family was there in their minivan, and my mom was right behind them in ours. Mrs. Rubinstein rolled down the window and waved me over.

"We walked King right before we left," she said. "He should be good for a few hours. We can't thank you enough, Grace. It's such a relief to know someone so conscientious is taking care of him."

Mrs. Rubinstein smiled so sincerely that I felt bad I'd had reluctant thoughts. "It's okay. Have a very nice trip," I said, and waved to Shoshi's dad in the driver's seat and to her sister, who was in back in a private earbud world.

When I got in next to my mom, she wanted to know if she should take me over to the Rubinsteins' immediately so I could get dog walking over with.

I rolled my eyes. "It doesn't work like that, Mom. Mrs. Rubinstein just walked him. I will walk him again after dinner."

"In the dark?" My mother was horrified.

"Mom, we live in the safest neighborhood in Massachusetts," I said. "Shoshi walks him herself all the time. Besides, he's very protective."

"Your father is going with you," Mom said, "and that's final."

I thought of many excuses to put off walking King after dinner, but at last my father had to insist because he was almost ready to "retire for the night."

"Thank you for coming with me," I said as we were putting on our jackets.

"Do you want to drive?" my dad asked.

"That's crazy," I said. "It's four blocks. Anyway, driving is bad for the climate."

My dad shrugged. "Suit yourself," he said.

As soon as we turned the corner onto the Rubinsteins'

block, I could hear King barking. He has a big bark to match his big self.

My father stopped walking. "Is that—" He looked at me warily.

I tugged his arm to get him moving. "Yes."

"He sounds as though he wants to eat us," my father said.

"You can wait outside," I said.

"What kind of father would I be if I sent my only child in there alone?"

Together we advanced onto the Rubinsteins' front porch. On his side of the door, King was in a frenzy— barking and jumping, his toenails *click-scratch*ing the wood. With every *thump*, my father flinched, and his fear made me scared. I knew how King behaved when Shoshi's family was home. But what if he was different when they weren't?

I couldn't turn back, though. I pretended to be brave for my father's sake.

"I'm going in," I announced.

"I will wait on the porch," my father said.

"What happened to how you're a bad dad if you don't come with me?" I asked.

"Someone has to be ready to call nine-one-one," he said.

I said, "Very funny," hoping it was a joke. Then I pushed the door open.

CHAPTER SIX

P.S.

Grace

King did not act different with the Rubinsteins gone. He was the same amount crazy as ever. The second I stepped in the door, he transformed from fearsome beast to lonely pal and overwhelmed me with affection.

"Okay, okay, King. Good dog. Glad to see you too," I said. "I'd wag my tail if I had one. *Bleah*—enough with the kisses! Come on, let's get ready to go."

King's leash was hanging on a hook in the hall closet. Corralling him and clipping it to his collar took a minute, but finally he was ready, and then he lunged to be free. He had been cooped up inside since three o'clock—more than five hours. If I had to go to the bathroom that badly, I guess I might lunge, too.

King ignored my dad on the porch, and shot right by him through the yard and out to the sidewalk—dragging me behind.

"Wait up!" my dad called, and he hustled along to catch us.

After watering a patch of grass by the street, King slowed down to a gallop. My father is normally a slow walker, so he had to work to keep up. King has very long legs, and Shoshi's family is taller than mine. It probably drove the poor dog crazy to be held back by such slowpokes.

On the trial walk when I visited on Thursday, I had noticed that King zigzags down the sidewalk, sniffing this fencepost or that bush with great urgency.

"Shoshi says it's his way of checking Facebook," I

explained. "He's getting status updates from his friends."

My dad nodded, as if accepting this as scientific fact. "So when he lifts his leg, that's the same as a 'like,'" he said.

"Yes, that must be right. Good thinking, Dad."

King's walk that night did not last long. Throughout it, I said to myself: *Just make sure he doesn't escape, and don't let him eat anything bad. Simple, right?*

Mrs. Rubinstein had told me ten minutes was enough, as long as he got a longer walk on Saturday morning. When we got back to the Rubinsteins' house, my dad came inside too. He had never been there before. I have been best friends with Shoshi for a year, but my parents hardly know her parents at all. I unclipped King's leash from his collar and put the leash away. Then I went into the kitchen to read the note Shoshi's mom had left for me.

Meanwhile, my dad was exploring. "They have quite an old TV," he observed.

"Da-a-a-ad!" I said.

"Of course," he continued, "they do have a son in college and two other children as well. Plus that dog probably costs a lot of money to feed. What do Shoshi's parents do for their professions, Grace?"

"Mr. Rubinstein is a lawyer, and Mrs. Rubinstein works for a nonprofit. But she only works part-time."

"Ah," said my father. "Now I understand."

"Understand what?" I said. King was following me around. The note from Shoshi's mom only had phone numbers and "Good luck" on it. I kind of wished they'd stop saying, "Good luck!" It seemed like they were afraid I was going to need it, which did not exactly make me feel confident.

"Why they live like they do," my dad said. "The old TV. The worn carpeting. They have too many expenses and not enough income. I hope they are saving adequately for retirement."

"For goodness' sake, Dad," I said. "It is none of your business, and the Rubinsteins are nice."

I got a puppy treat out of the canister on the kitchen counter. King was whining and wagging his tail he was so excited about the puppy treat. You would have thought he was starving. "Good dog.

Here you go. See you tomorrow. Sleep tight," I said.

I was hoping the treat would distract King from our leaving, but it occupied him for less than a second. When I looked back before I closed the door, he was watching my dad and me with big lonely eyes. Poor guy. He was used to noise and people around all the time. This must be strange for him.

As we walked home, I lectured my dad. "Shoshi is my best friend. Not everyone has to make a lot of money or work all the time or have the best TV."

"Their refrigerator was old too," my dad persisted.

"Some people would say you and Mom shouldn't work so much," I said.

At that my father hesitated a half step. He was surprised. "But your mother and I always come to your recitals," he said.

"I wasn't talking about me," I said. "You should have a hobby. You should read more. You and Mom should go to the movies." I would never have said these things except I was annoyed by my father's comments about Shoshi's house.

"I don't know anything but work, Grace. Maybe it is all I am good for," Dad said.

Now I felt terrible. I hadn't meant to say anything mean.

It was dark and there are no streetlights in our neighborhood. I couldn't see my dad's face, but when he spoke, he sounded sad, and for some reason I thought of King's big eyes.

"You're good at being a dad," I said. I took his hand, something I probably hadn't done since I needed help crossing the street. "You were ready to protect me from the big vicious beast."

"That is true," my dad said. "Do you really think I need a hobby? What hobby would I choose?"

"I will have to think about that," I said.

CHAPTER SEVEN

Grace

It was seven fifteen when I went downstairs the next morning. I grabbed a Pop-Tart for strength, wrote a note to remind my parents where I was, and headed out the door. I would take King for a long walk now and a shorter one later on.

By now maybe King knew the sound of my footsteps, or else he could smell me through the door. Whatever it was, he only barked once—more like a hello yelp—as I came up the walk. King must be a fast learner, I thought. I'm a fast learner too.

When I opened the Rubinsteins' door, I was greeted with a rush of tail-wagging joy. It was a lot of enthusiasm to take in so early in the morning, but after the first shock it felt good. Is this why people have dogs?

The day was clear and sunny, but the nighttime coolness lingered. I was glad I'd put on my red MIT sweatshirt. MIT stands for Massachusetts Institute of Technology. That's where my parents want me to go to college.

King was thrilled to be outside and made frequent stops to check Facebook.

A cat ran in front of us. King tugged and barked. A rabbit ran across a yard, and King tugged and barked again. We passed a dead crow in the street, and King showed an interest I thought was unhealthy. Then Mr. Hackman came around the corner with his little white poodle, and King got very excited.

Uh-oh, I thought. *Does that poodle come under the Rubinsteins' heading "foods King is not supposed to eat"?*

I pulled back on the leash just in case, but Mr. Hackman told me not to worry. "That's King, isn't it?" he said. "He and my dog, Bruiser, get along just fine. Are the Rubinsteins out of town?"

I explained while King bent down and got nose to nose with Bruiser—then nose to other body parts too. It was gross, and my face must have revealed my opinion because Mr. Hackman laughed. "That's just doggy conversation, Grace. Come on, Bruiser. Enough with the gossip. You have a good day now."

"Yes, sir," I said. "I will."

Back at the Rubinsteins', I looked at the kitchen clock and saw it was almost eight thirty. We had been walking one whole hour!

Before lunch, I went to Chinese class and ballet as usual. Mrs. Lun picks me up from Chinese and Lily's dad from ballet, so I had said only hi-bye to my parents till my mom and I sat down at the kitchen counter to eat. I had a bologna sandwich on white bread with mayonnaise. She had canned tomato soup.

"According to your father," Mom said, "you were very brave with that big dog last night."

"I didn't have to be brave really. He is just enthusiastic, like Shoshi told me. I was worried for nothing," I said.

"They should be paying you," my mom said.

Not this again! "It's a *favor*," I said. "Doing favors is generous. You're always telling me I should learn to be generous."

"Not that generous," my mom said.

"I kind of like walking King," I said. "I think we should get a dog too. How about a Siberian husky? They are huge and furry."

My mother's eyes got big, and she put down her soup spoon.

I continued. "A dog would make me more well-rounded. I bet everyone who gets into MIT has one."

"Do you really think so, Grace?" my mother asked.

I laughed. "Mom! I'm teasing! I know you and Dad don't do pets. But I am telling the truth about King. Walking him isn't that bad."

After lunch, I went back to the Rubinsteins'. This was the walk I was dreading because by now King would definitely need to "do his business," as Shoshi called it—in other words, poop. The Rubinsteins' leash had a plastic cylinder attached, and inside it were blue plastic bags especially designed for containing it.

I wonder if the kids whose parents work in the factories that make these bags are embarrassed on career day when they introduce their parents and say what their jobs are.

About two blocks from home, King stopped abruptly to sniff and then started circling. "What's up?" I asked, but I had a feeling I knew, and sure enough, as if he was answering, he squatted.

"Got it," I said. Then I looked up at the leaves of the maple trees, which were just beginning to turn red. Even dogs deserve their privacy.

King tugged at the leash a few moments later, ready to move on as if nothing had happened. I wished I could do that too, but it wouldn't be conscientious. So many people have dogs that if we all ignored the obvious, the world would soon be heaped in dog poop. So I was a good citizen and bent down and picked up the deposit the way Shoshi had demonstrated, with my hand wrapped in plastic. All the time I held my breath and tried not to think about what I was holding.

King, meanwhile, looked back quizzically, like what could possibly be taking so long?

I felt embarrassed to be carrying dog poop after that. I kind of hoped no one would see me. I was thinking of washing my hands, how good the soapy water would feel, when it happened. Strange, huh? A whole disaster resulted from me imagining clean hands.

CHAPTER EIGHT

Grace

Our development is pretty big so I cannot know everybody, and I did not know the people who live at 123 Farmers Lane. That day they were getting a grocery delivery, and the green van was in their driveway with the back doors open. The driver wasn't there. He must've gone around back with a big load of groceries. All this I only halfway noticed as King and I walked toward the driveway, me with the bag of dog poop, looking forward to washing my hands.

I have thought so hard about what happened next, I have basically done crime scene reconstruction. At the time, though, it was a blur.

King was trotting a few steps ahead of me. A good dog walker, a conscientious one, would have seen that his ears were up. Something had interested him. I should have watched extra carefully. But I did not watch until all at once I felt the leash jerk powerfully, and its plastic grip yanked painfully at my knuckles.

Then my arm dropped abruptly, but it was a few moments before my poor brain processed what had happened. King had pulled the leash loose. He was gone and sprinting toward the van in the driveway. A second later, he was out of my sight behind it.

I yelled at him and ran. I am pretty fast, but he was a dog on a mission. By the time I caught up, King was surrounded by havoc and destruction. Chewed plastic on the ground, white frosting on his nose, and the scent of sugar and spices everywhere.

My heart sank, and my plan changed. Get King. Get away. Keep Grace Xi out of trouble!

First I stomped on King's leash so he couldn't go anywhere, then I picked up the plastic grip, and then I tugged him away from the rest of the groceries. I was mad, but King was puzzled. Was it his fault someone had left a massive dog treat unprotected? What did I expect a dog to do, anyway?

There was a fence along the driveway of 123 Farmers Lane, and this turned out to be lucky. Once we were back on the sidewalk, we made a fast left turn and were out of sight behind it. Only a moment passed till I heard footsteps and talking—the delivery driver returning from the backyard: "Two twenty Locust, Dunstable—okay. One fifteen p.m., I'll be—oh *sheesh!* What happened here?"

My heart jumped into my throat. He had seen the mess! What if he came looking for its cause? For a second I felt weak all over. Then I forced myself to run. King thought this was a game and galloped gleefully ahead of me. Soon we were far from the scene of the crime.

King was in an especially good mood after that and

wanted to stop and leave messages on every blade of grass. I imagined him bragging to his friends about escaping his captor and eating the carrot cake. For a dog, it had to be one big triumph.

As for me, I felt sick and wanted to be done with dogs forever.

Back at the Rubinsteins', I realized I still had the blue plastic bag. I dropped it in the trash can outdoors, gave King his food and water, and put the leash back on the hook. In other words, I became the perfect and conscientious dog walker that Shoshi's family expected me to be.

But all the time I was thinking of one thing, one gross thing I never expected to think about in my life, and that was dog digestion. Could King's insides process all that sugar and fat?

I should call the vet. I should call Shoshi's mom. But if I did, it would be admitting to everyone that I, Grace Xi, had messed up. I might even have to go back to 123 Farmers Lane and tell this to total strangers.

I knew I could never do that.

And besides, King himself seemed happy—which so entirely was not fair. What had happened was his fault, not mine. Why did he look so guiltless?

Needless to say, there was no puppy treat for King that day. Instead, I knelt and looked straight into his face. "You are a bad dog," I said solemnly.

King did not believe this for one minute. He wagged his tail. He lolled his tongue. His breath still smelled like frosting.

CHAPTER NINE

Grace

I had wanted to write Lucy back immediately, but she was right, I am busy. Between walking King twice more and finishing my project on ancient Rome, I didn't have time to sit down at my desk until late Sunday afternoon.

Sunday, Sept. 24

Dear Lucy,

   Thank you for your letter. It was very
nice to hear from you. Please congratulate
Kendall for me about the new baby. I hope
your mom and the officer are still happy.
While I am hoping, I will go ahead and hope
your grandmother is also happy even though
you did not mention her very much.

   You are right that I am busy, but I am
also fine except for one thing. My stomach
has been hurting since yesterday.

   Perhaps you did not know that I have
a bad stomach. It hurts most when I am
worried. What I am worried about now is
that I messed up when I was walking my
friend Shoshi's dog while her family was out
of town, and he ran away from me. I know

you and Olivia and Emma think I am good
at everything, but I am not good at dog
walking.

Shoshi's family got back from their
trip today, and they brought me a Lake
Winnipesaukee T-shirt to say thank you for
walking King. This made my stomach hurt
even more.

A little while ago, things got worse.

Shoshi called and said King was sick. I
am sorry to have to put this word in a
letter, but just to explain, he has diarrhea.
Everywhere. Shoshi asked if anything unusual
happened while they were gone.

Of course I said no. I couldn't tell the
truth then when I hadn't told them in the
first place. That would have been like two
mess-ups!

Now my parents are asking why I am "mopey"
and don't want dinner and why I am not being
nice to them either. I never realized before

how much easier it is to be good at everything.

I am sorry to be writing so much. I would not blame you if you already got bored and stopped reading.

So anyway, if flour power is supposed to solve problems, I need it to fix my stomach and keep me from messing up any more.

Love you always-your failure of a friend,

Grace Xi

P.S. If it matters, the new baby at Vivek's house is a girl. Even though we broke up, we are still friends on Facebook. You should be his friend too. I don't mind. I think he always liked you better than me anyway, like most boys do. Who wouldn't?

King recovered. No one from 123 Farmers Lane or the grocery delivery company came to the door to ask me questions.

Even so, I was in a bad mood all week, and my stomach barely got better. At school, my friends wanted to know why I was so quiet, and I just shrugged. At home, Snot-Nosed Grace took over every conversation with my parents. Wednesday at dinner we were eating take-out pizza, and I complained that the crust was soggy because—hello-o-o-o?—the crust *was* soggy.

Is a person allowed to speak the truth once in a while?

My parents put down their forks. I thought I would soon hear a lecture about the importance of being grateful for everything I have, but instead my parents looked at each other, and then they looked at me. Their faces were sympathetic, which was much worse than if their faces had been annoyed.

"What?" I said.

My father cleared his throat. "Grace," he said, "your mother and I believe that you are growing up."

"I hope so," I said. "I wouldn't want to be this short forever."

My father breathed in and out. "What I mean," he

said, "is that your body is changing. And these changes are caused by chemicals called hormones—"

OMG. Was this about to become the Talk—the one where your parents try to tell you about boys and s-e-x and babies?

"—that travel through your body, everyone's bodies, in fact, and these chemicals—"

"*Dad!*" I interrupted. "I *know* all this! What do you think gym teachers are for?"

My father paused. My parents looked at each other again.

"I thought they taught you the rules of volleyball and golf and lacrosse," my mother said.

I rolled my eyes. Neither of my parents had gone to school in the United States. As smart as they are, there is a lot they don't understand. I try to be patient.

"They teach body stuff, too," I said, "so parents don't have to. *Seriously. You don't have to*."

"And you don't have to be rude," said my father.

"We are only trying to help," said my mother.

"Lately you have been rude about many things," said

my father. "This is not like you, Grace. We assumed it was the hormones."

I took a breath. Then I closed my eyes and scrunched up my face and blew out my bangs. *They are trying to help,* I reminded myself. *It's not their fault that they are parents.* "I will try to be less rude," I said.

"Is something the matter?" my mother asked. "Are your grades okay?"

"Of course nothing's the matter," I said. "Of course my grades are fine."

CHAPTER TEN

Grace

The next Saturday when I came home from karate and ballet, both my parents were waiting in the kitchen and so—on the counter—was a square package addressed to me.

"We think it is from your friend Lucy," said my mother. "The return address is Beverly Hills."

"We think it must be cookies," said my father.

"Aren't you going to open it now?" My mother handed me a knife.

My parents claim they don't care about food, but obviously they do care about cookies. This is something we have in common. I keep a private stash of Oreos in my room for emergencies. And Lucy's homemade cookies, like Hannah's, are even better than Oreos.

When I took the knife and cut the tape on the box, I was surprised that I did not smell a wonderful smell. I was even more surprised when I looked at the cookie tin inside and saw a note on top: WARNING! DO NOT EAT!

My father read this and tilted his head to one side. "That is very strange," he said.

Confused, I removed the lid of the tin and took a look at the actual cookies. They were small, dry-looking, and dotted with oats—nothing like the delicious, sparkling lemon cookies from Hannah or the chocolate chip cookies Lucy sent last year.

My disappointed parents shook their heads and sighed. "Something must be wrong with Lucy's oven," said my father.

"Or perhaps she doesn't like you anymore, Grace," said my mother. "Did you do something to offend her?"

"No, of course not," I said, but I was as baffled as my parents and almost as disappointed. Then I thought of something. I picked up a cookie and sniffed. All of a sudden it felt like I was back at the Rubinsteins' with King.

"It's a dog cookie!" I said. "A dog biscuit, I mean. In my letter, I told Lucy I was taking care of King."

"Ah." My father nodded. "So she made cookies for the Rubinsteins' dog. That is peculiar but better, I guess, than her not liking you, or her having a broken oven."

"I think we should remember to buy cookies next time we go to the store," my mother said.

"They won't be the same as homemade," my father said. "Grace, wouldn't you like to make some cookies for your family? Don't you have to make a practice batch for your secret club? It's about time for you to send some to Emma, is it not?"

"How do you even know that?" I asked. "You're not supposed to know about the club at all."

"We know because you told us," my mother said.

"Are we supposed to forget?" my father asked.

"Yes," I said. "No. Oh, I don't know. Anyway, there's a letter with the dog biscuits, and I am going up to my room to read it."

"Don't you want some lunch?" my mother said.

"Later," I said, already on the stairs.

In my room, I kicked off my sneakers, sat on my bed, and leaned back against the reading pillow. As usual, Lucy had written on lined paper ripped out of a spiral notebook, not stationery or cards like I have for notes. This paper made me wonder again what her life at home was like. Did she keep her room messy (like Shoshi) or neat (like me)? Did her mom and grandma let her hang up whatever she wanted on her bedroom walls? Did she make her own bed in the morning, or did her mom do it?

I was glad to have Lucy's letter, but I reminded myself I was also a little bit mad at her. It was partly for sending dog cookies. It was partly for asking about Vivek and reminding me that I am jealous of her. I shouldn't be jealous of my friend, right? But deep in my heart, I couldn't help it.

I am not a perfect person. But I guess you already know that, right? I can't even walk a dog.

Carefully, I slit the envelope open with my fingernail, pulled out the letter, and read.

Hi, Grace—

I was going to make more cookies, some for King and some for humans, but Kendall had the baby early, and her mom was in Europe, and her husband was traveling on business, and I had to go over and help wrangle triplets, and there was no time.

So far (Day 4) Piper is a terrible baby. I have to remind myself that it is not her fault she is a baby and that all babies cry, but do all babies cry all the time?

My mom says I never cried. My nana
says my mom doesn't remember whether
I did or not because my mom was too busy
with her own shenanigans to pay her
only daughter much mind, whatever that
means.

Anyway, perversely (that is a word I
learned from my nana), the triplets are
being extra unusually helpful—even Levi.
Sometimes he looks down at his tiny, red,
screaming sister and shakes his head
and says, "Poor sad little baby."

So anyway, these cookies are for King
because your stomach will feel better
if you give them to him. It will be like
an apology for messing up. I think Shoshie
will forgive you.

Which reminds me (change of topic):
The case of the dead computer has been
solved! After some tough questions from
Officer Leonard, Nana admitted she had

spilled a cup of tea on the keyboard, causing it to—zzzzzzzt!!!—fry in its own electricity. Nana denies that she did this on purpose. I don't think I believe her. Anyway, it looks like it will be a while before I have e-mail or the Internet or any of those other modern conveniences . . . except when I'm at school.

I would explain more if I had more time, but Kendall just called and Arlo and Mia are singing lullabies extra loud to drown out crying, and Kendall is tearing her hair, so she wants me to PLEASE come over, and I am going.

Love ya

—Lucy

P.S. Are you a little bit mad at me for mentioning Vivek? Sorry.

When I finished reading Lucy's letter, I was so mad that I started to tear it up.

But after one corner I stopped.

It was kind of freaky how Lucy knew from almost three thousand miles away that I was a little bit mad at her. Did it mean she knew about other stuff, too? Did it mean she was right that Shoshi would forgive me?

CHAPTER ELEVEN

Grace

That afternoon, instead of doing math homework for my tutor, I made raspberry thumbprint cookies for my parents and me. If I had been doing anything else, my parents would have nagged me to work on homework. As it was, they didn't say a thing, just hung around the kitchen more than usual.

The cookies on the first sheet came out too brown. My mother looked at them, shook her head, and declared that she would wait for the next ones.

My father said, "If they are dry, who cares? I can always drink more milk."

The first cookies did taste a little toasty, but the second batch was good enough even for my mother. She poured us milk, and all three of us ate warm cookies while sitting at the kitchen counter. Here is something you should know about raspberry thumbprint cookies. If you don't have enough self-control to wait a few minutes for them to cool, the hot jam burns your mouth.

"Are you going to send the rest of these to Emma?" my father asked. There was a spot of jam at the corner of his mouth, which my mother dabbed off with a paper napkin. My parents are gross like that sometimes. I try to ignore it.

"I have to write to Emma first and see what she needs cookies for," I said. "After that, I send them. Hannah's cookies were sort of different. She's not really part of the club. It's for campers, and she's a counselor. She's old."

My father nodded and said, "I see. Now am I supposed to forget you told me that as well?"

"Yes," I said, "and add another thing to the list of what I'm not good at: keeping secrets."

"What do you mean 'another thing'?" my mother asked.

"You are good at most things, Grace," my father said. "You should tell us what it is that's been bothering you, and then you will feel better. That's what families are for."

"That and to encourage you to work hard and behave properly," said my mother.

My father frowned.

My mother raised her eyebrows. "What?"

"We will talk later," said my father.

"I want to talk now," said my mother.

I hopped down from the stool. "You guys go ahead and sort this out. I am going over to Shoshi's."

Perversely, as Lucy's nana would say, it was talking to my parents that convinced me I ought to tell Shoshi the truth. This is not as crazy as it sounds. Talking to them made me realize that I did want to tell someone. It also made me realize I did not want my parents to be the someone.

I put the cookies and dog biscuits in a shopping bag. I put on a jacket. Outside, the sky had clouded up, and wind gusts made the falling leaves fly. I heard a crow complain about something, but when I looked up I couldn't find him. I rehearsed what I was going to say: Shoshi, I am sorry, but I messed up when I was walking King. I was thinking about washing my hands, and he got away. He ate a whole cake. It was a carrot cake, so I hope it had healthy vitamins. I am really sorry.

I said this over and over till I had it memorized. But on Shoshi's porch, it went clean out of my head. Something was wrong, but only after I rang the doorbell did I figure out what: There was no dog barking.

Shoshi opened the door for me. "Oh, hey, Grace, hi. Come on in." When I did, I have to tell you it was a strange sensation to walk into the Rubinsteins' front hall without being jumped on and licked.

"Where's King?" I asked.

Shoshi answered as we walked back toward the family room. The TV was on and the Patriots were playing.

"At the vet," she said. "He's really sick. They have to keep him overnight."

"Really sick, uh . . . how exactly?" I asked.

"Dehydrated, the vet said—like all the diarrhea and vomit and everything dried him out too much. Plus we found some plastic in his poop, and it might have hurt his insides. Sorry for the TMI. When you have a dog, you kind of get used to it. Anyway, my mom says the bill is going to be so big we'll be living on baked beans for a month."

Shoshi sat down on the couch. I sat down next to her. All the time I was thinking, *Oh no, oh no, oh no!*

And I couldn't be sure, but had Shoshi looked at me funny? Did she already know it was my fault her dog was sick? That I had messed up?

"He'll be fine, though, won't he?" I held up the bag. "I brought him some dog biscuits. Lucy made them for him."

Shoshi wrinkled her forehead. "Lucy-from-camp Lucy? Why would she make King dog biscuits?"

This was my moment! Cue the big speech! But before

I could suck in a breath and begin, Shoshi's mom came in. "What's the score—oh, hi, Grace. So that was you at the door. What's in the bag?"

"Dog biscuits!" Shoshi answered for me. "Weird, huh?"

"A get-well gift? That's very kind of you, Grace," Mrs. Rubinstein said.

"There are people cookies too," I said.

"I'll pick up milk at the store," said Mrs. Rubinstein. "Do we need anything else, Shosh? I'm just leaving."

Shoshi shrugged. "Guacamole maybe? For the second half?"

"Not in the budget," said Mrs. Rubinstein. "Maybe we can afford the store brand of salsa. Back in a few, girls. Thanks for the cookies, Grace."

Mrs. Rubinstein left through the door to the garage. Now I knew I couldn't hesitate or I would never have the courage to tell Shoshi at all. I heard the squeak of the electric garage door opener, and I started my speech: "Shoshi, I am sorry, but I messed up when I was walking King. . . ."

When I was done, the TV was showing a commercial for car insurance. Other than the announcer, Shoshi's family room was quiet, and every second I waited for her to say something made my stomach feel worse. I was afraid I might even vomit—and how embarrassing would *that* be? Then Shoshi looked at me and said, "You had better go home, Grace, before I say something really mean. Go—do you hear me? But leave the cookies for us."

My face was burning as I exited; the walk home seemed very long. All the time I was thinking one thing: *Lucy was wrong.* The truth was a big mistake.

CHAPTER TWELVE

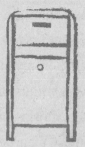

Sunday, October 16, Emma

My great-grandmother died on a Sunday. GG—that's what we called her—was in the hospital because she caught a lung infection at the assisted-living place where she lived. We all thought she was getting better, but all of a sudden she got worse, and then overnight she was gone. Early that morning, my grandmother (GG's daughter) called my mother (GG's granddaughter) to tell her.

My family—Mom, Dad, brother Benjamin, and me—were all in the kitchen when my mom answered her phone, and from her side of the conversation we could tell right away what had happened.

For a moment after my mom hung up, she stared straight ahead, like she couldn't see what was in front of her.

My dad said, "Darling, she was ninety. People don't live forever."

This made my mom frown, and my brother said, "You're not being helpful, Dad. Can I have some cereal?"

"Ben!" I scolded him. Wasn't cereal disrespectful?

"Wherever GG is, she wants me to have cereal," Benjamin said. "She knows I am a growing boy."

My mom held her arms out. Benjamin gave her a hug. When he squirmed free, I got him some cereal. He was probably right that GG would have wanted me to. Meanwhile, Dad opened the bag of coffee, scooped a scoop of grounds, and spilled them all over the floor.

"Do we have a broom?" he asked.

"Yes, Dad. In the broom closet," I said.

"Imagine that," Dad said, but instead of getting the broom, he went back to making coffee.

"Benjamin, get the broom," I said.

"Why do I have—," he started to say, but then he saw the look on my face and changed his mind. "Okay."

"Uh, Mom, do you want some cereal?" I asked.

Mom didn't answer. Ike, our ancient golden retriever, ambled over and sat in front of her and looked up into her face, trying to figure out what was going on.

"Sweetheart?" my dad said to my mom once the coffee was burbling. "I am very sorry about GG."

"Mom?" I said.

At last my mother looked up. "What?" she said.

"Dad's talking to you," I said. "So am I."

"Grandma will be here soon," she said. "There's a lot to do. I'm just going to go upstairs and wash my face."

Ben finished sweeping up the coffee. I said thank you, then looked at my dad. "Mom's acting a little weird," I said. "Don't you think? She ought to eat."

"She's fine," he said. "She has to be."

My family is Jewish, and Jews believe you're supposed to bury someone as soon as possible after they die. This meant that day the grown-ups had a lot of stuff to do in a hurry. Ben and I tried alternately to stay out of the way or be available "to be good helpers."

Besides making phone calls and doing errands, the adults took turns going to the funeral home to sit in a special room with GG. This is another Jewish tradition. Until the burial, the body cannot be left alone.

"How was it?" Ben asked my dad when he got back from his shift Sunday evening.

"Peaceful," my dad said.

"Were you afraid of ghosts?" Ben said. "You know it's almost Halloween, right?"

"Afraid of your GG's ghost?" my dad said. "Not at all. In fact, I dozed off."

"Is that allowed?" I asked.

"No one told me it wasn't," my dad said. "Anyway, GG was such a good person I'm sure nothing I did would hurt her standing with God any. He'll blame me, not her, for any faux pas."

"A 'faux pas' is a mistake," I told Ben. He's in fourth grade.

"I knew that," said Ben.

"No, you didn't," I said.

"I did too," said Ben.

"Kids?" said my dad.

"Sorry," we said.

The next day, Monday, Ben and I stayed home from school, my mom took off work, and my dad came home early. To keep from getting behind, I did homework, which actually felt good because it felt normal.

At lunchtime, I tried to convince my mom to eat a turkey sandwich, but she said she wasn't hungry. She was pacing around the first floor of our house with earbuds in her ears so she could talk on the phone. I had caught her on a lap through the kitchen. I think she was on hold.

"Okay, I'll make myself a turkey sandwich." I opened the refrigerator and got out turkey, mayonnaise, and cheese. On my mom's next lap through the kitchen, I looked up. "Mom? I'm worried I don't feel sad enough about GG."

"Feel sad—what?" She stopped and looked at me. I could tell she was also listening in case the person on the other end of the phone line picked up. "Oh, that's okay, Emma. Don't be worried," she said. "You can be sad later. That's my plan."

"I know—how about peanut butter?" I said. "You love peanut butter."

Mom raised one finger, meaning hang on a sec. The call was something to do with GG's credit card bill. Then, reciting a bunch of numbers, she turned away from me and walked into the family room.

My family includes several people who have died—three grandparents and one brother, Nathan. Before GG, though, they all passed away either before I was born or when I was too little to understand.

From GG I learned that dying is really complicated.

We left for the temple at three thirty. The service was at four. I couldn't believe how many people came! Who were they, anyway? How had GG known them? She had always said that all her friends were dead.

After the rabbi said the prayers, anyone who wanted

to could come up to the front and say nice things.

My grandmother, my mother, and my aunt spoke first, and then it was my turn. I was wearing a blue dress we bought last year. It was a little bit shorter than it used to be, and a little snugger, too. My mother and I both hate to shop. My grandmother is different. She has fashion sense. I could feel her eyes on me as I stood in front of everybody, and I could read her brain waves, too. She wished she had taken me shopping for something nice to wear to the service.

"My GG taught me Yiddish," I said, trying not to think about my too-snug dress. "It was the language she spoke growing up in Europe. She would squeeze my cheeks and say 'schoene punim.' That means 'cute face.' She used to 'kvell' over my brother, which means say how great he was, and 'kvetch' about her bad memory, which means complain.

"My GG was almost always cheerful," I concluded. "Even though her family had to escape the Nazis in Europe and come to the United States when she was a little girl, she stayed optimistic and kind."

My grandmother might have been unhappy about my dress, but she still squeezed my hand and whispered, "Very nice, Emma," when I sat down next to her.

Benjamin got up after me and said that GG had been proud of him for playing hockey even though she had never been to one of his games because for her there would have been too much noise and hubbub. "Someday when I have great-grandchildren," he said, "I will treat them just like GG treated Emma and me."

CHAPTER THIRTEEN

Emma

The following Monday, the eighth day after GG died, Hannah's lemon cookies came in the mail.

I know it was the eighth day because our family had just finished sitting shivah. "Shivah" means "seven" in Hebrew, and sitting shivah means you spend seven days being sad at home and saying prayers to honor the dead person's memory.

Other traditions go with it too, like you cover up your mirrors because compared to death and eternity, your looks are not supposed to be important. Also, instead of flowers, your friends bring you food. We Jews don't believe that flowers go well with funerals. Our idea is it's bad enough that a person had to die, so why should flowers have to die too?

My family did not follow the shivah rules exactly. For example, after the first Monday, we didn't stay home from work and school. My dad is a doctor, and my mom is a lawyer. Their patients and clients need them.

Ben, of course, was totally in favor of skipping school, but my parents wouldn't let him. "What if we get in trouble with the rabbi?" Ben argued. "What if we get in trouble with God?"

"The rabbi believes in learning, and so does God, and so did your great-grandmother," my mother said. "You are going to school."

We did do some things right. We said the Kaddish prayers—those are the ones especially for the dead—and in the evenings family and friends came over. Everyone brought delicious food. My mother still wasn't eating.

The package from Hannah was waiting on our front porch that Monday when I got home from school. I picked it up, let myself in, dropped my backpack on the floor, and called, "Hello?" I knew Ben was at hockey practice, and my parents were at work, but Ike was in his usual spot, stretched out on the floor in the kitchen. Ike used to run to the door barking and dancing when I got home, but now the best he can do is raise his head and thump his tail.

"Everyone gets old, huh, Ike?" I bent down and scratched him behind his ears. "You're still a good dog—yes, you are."

A package the size of a shoe box from Hannah could only mean one thing, and I was hungry. It took about five seconds for me to scissor the cardboard open. Amazingly, I did not scissor myself.

In the box—tucked like treasure under layers of plastic and wax paper—were a whole lot of perfectly formed, frosted lemon cookies.

Yum!

Did I mention I was hungry?

In health class this year, we learned about EQ, which is like IQ only for emotions. If you have a high EQ, you do the right thing even when you don't really want to. I knew that the right thing to do that instant was eat something healthy and save the cookies to share with my family after dinner.

Ha!

But I did compromise. I poured a glass of milk, put two cookies on a plate, and sat down at the kitchen table. Maybe if I read Hannah's letter at the same time, I would eat slower.

Oct. 19

Dear Emma,

I am on a lemon cookie spree!

This happens to me sometimes.

I find a recipe I like, and I make it over and over. Grace said these cookies were very popular at her house, and that is a direct quote. You know how formal Grace is sometimes. She cracks me up.

I hope everything is wonderful for you and your family.

To tell you the truth, though, this semester has been tough for your old counselor—me.

Emphasis on the OLD!!!

Since the beginning of summer when Travis dumped me till right now today when Jack wants me back so he can just go and smash my heart again, I feel like I have aged about one century.

You already know about Travis, right? I had the feeling you four campers sussed out that piece of heartbreak last summer even though I am sure I never said a word.

What happened with Jack is after we broke up he wanted me back but I said no, and then I had to tell him to stop texting so often because we were broken up. (Hello? What is it about broken up that you don't understand?) Then he wanted to know how often was too often? and I said once a week would be okay. So now he texts every Monday morning at either 7 a.m. (if he gets up when his alarm goes off) or noon (if he sleeps through it).

Here is a typical text: I love you, Hannah. Whoever he is, I might be fatter but I am also funnier. I promise I will make you laugh every day and twice on Sunday. By the way, I have been working out.

Gross, right? Besides, who wants to go through life laughing all the time? Some of us are serious people with serious things to do like study.

And besides, there is no "whoever." I mean, I am not a nun. I go out and talk to people who happen to be male, but that doesn't count as a "whoever," does it? A "whoever" would have to be one "whoever" that I liked better than Jack, and there is no "whoever" like that currently in my life. It's true that sometimes I do see Travis around, and he looks all like a sad puppy, and I hear he broke up with that other girl he was seeing after me.

My apologies, Emma, if this is TMI. But if you learn now what boys are like it will save you trouble later.

Not that there's any boy trouble for me anymore. Like I said, everything is totally fine. As my grandpa would have said: With flour power, what could be bad?

Best always and take care and don't worry too much because I know how you are.

—Hannah

P.S. Sorry to be so boring. Other than dumb boys, things are
fine, and I am getting smarter in my classes about art and
art history. Are you looking forward to horse sweat and summer
sunshine yet?

P.P.S. I always remember to wear sunscreen!

That last P.S. made me smile. Hannah was teasing
me. Around camp I am well-known for reminding my
friends about sunscreen.

To keep from eating more cookies, I closed up the
box and put it in the refrigerator, and—while I was in
there anyway—got out some baby carrots.

Something about the letter was bugging me. I had
to chew two carrots before I figured it out: Hannah
was complaining about boys, and—at a time like
this—boys seemed kind of (no offense, Hannah) silly.

I swallowed. I ate another carrot.

On the other hand, there was this crazy long speech
Olivia had delivered one day at camp last summer.

It mentioned flower girls and proms and poets and princesses. In the end, the point—I think—was that humans need romance, or else humans will all go extinct.

Looked at like that, boy trouble isn't silly at all.

CHAPTER FOURTEEN

Emma

There were plenty of lemon cookies left for dessert. After dinner, while my parents, Ben, and I were still at the table, I put some on a plate. My dad took two and my mom took one. Ben sniffed and shook his head.

"They smell weird," he said.

I pulled the plate away. "More for me."

"Wait." He reached for a cookie and inspected it. "I *guess* I'll try one."

"Don't do me any favors," I said.

"Who's Hannah again?" my dad asked. "Why is she sending us cookies?"

My dad's brain is so full of important medical stuff that regular life gets crowded out. My mother is different. She can name all the girls in Flowerpot Cabin and all their parents, too. She probably even remembers what Hannah is studying in college. Now I expected her to set my dad straight. She usually likes showing off that way. But she didn't. She had resumed that staring look from the morning she found out about GG.

I explained about Hannah to my dad. Meanwhile my mother ate one bite of cookie.

"I'll finish your cookie for you," Ben told her after she'd put it down.

"Don't let him, Mom! You need it," I said.

"I'm going to bed." Mom stood up. "See you in the morning."

Ben ate the cookie. Then the two of us did dishes as usual and watched TV in the family room. After I went upstairs and got ready for bed, I came back down and found my dad in his office at the end of the hall.

"Hello, sweetie," he said when I walked in. "Did you come to say good night? How nice."

"Partly," I said, "but I also have a question. Is Mom sick, do you think?"

"I doubt it," he said. "She rarely gets sick."

"Is she upset about GG?" I asked.

My dad has one of those fancy swivel desk chairs. Now he rolled his shoulders and leaned back in it. "Of course she is," he said. "It has been a busy time and a sad one. But GG had made her peace with life, and your mom knows that. GG was ready for whatever comes next."

"I miss her," I said. "Even though we didn't see her every day, just knowing she's not there anymore . . . I miss her. But I haven't cried. Is that weird?"

Dad shrugged. "People are sad in different ways, Emma. You will cry on your own schedule. Now, may I have that kiss? I've got a couple more things to read here before I go up to bed."

My dad's cheek was scratchy like always. I knew

when he said a couple more things that he'd be in his office for hours. I hoped my mom was okay.

A sound woke me in the middle of the night, but it was familiar, not scary. Someone was tapping on my door.

"You can come in," I said softly.

The doorknob turned, the door opened, and my little brother padded across the rug. "Em? Do you think GG can see us?" he asked.

"Of course not," I said. "Go back to bed."

"Oh," Ben said. "Okay."

"Wait," I said. "I don't know if she can or not. I never thought of it before."

"If she can, then maybe she can protect us," he said.

"I guess," I said. "Do we need protecting especially?"

"Everybody needs protecting," Benjamin said, "like from bigger kids."

I had been lying on my back. Now I rolled over and propped myself up on an elbow. I wished it weren't the middle of the night. I wished I weren't so sleepy. "Are bigger kids bothering you, Ben?"

"They might," he said. "We had a bullying unit."

"Everyone had a bullying unit," I said, and then I had a funny thought. "In the bullying unit, did they mention asking ghosts for protection?"

"Not exactly," Ben said. "Do you think GG is a ghost now?"

"I guess so," I said. "But they're kind of fuzzy on that part in Hebrew school."

"If she is, she can haunt the big kids," said Ben.

"GG wasn't very scary," I said. "Grandma would be better at haunting."

"She isn't going to die too—is she?" Ben asked.

"Probably not yet," I said. "She goes to yoga and to spin class. Aren't you getting sleepy by now?"

"If she needed to help me out, GG would haunt the big kids. I'm pretty sure," said Benjamin.

"I'm pretty sure too," I said.

"Good night, Em," Ben said.

"Good night."

* * *

It was the next day—Tuesday—that I started to worry for real about my mom. She stayed home from work. And she stayed home from Ben's hockey scrimmage, too.

Last hockey season, my brother was puny and didn't play much. This year he's still puny but he's fast. Grandma says he inherited all the coordination in the family, which, if you think about it, is another way to say that I inherited no coordination. Either way, my parents and I almost always go to see his team play.

I don't admit this to Ben, but it's fun. Sports on TV are boring, but when your own brother is playing and you know the other kids, too, it's exciting to see them do well and awful to see them mess up.

Late that afternoon Dad went to the game by himself, and I stayed home in case Mom needed anything. I was doing geometry in my room when my phone signaled I had a text. I expected it to be from either my friend Caitlin or else Kayden, the third-grader I tutor after school. Instead it was from Grace Xi—one of my bunkmates from summer camp.

Grace: Cookies coming soon! How R U?

Me: Oh, tx! K but my GG died.

Grace: ☹ What is GG?

Me: Great-grandmother.

Grace: 😣 Flour power not enough.

Wait—flower power, what? I thought about this for a second, then realized she was saying death could not be fixed by flour power, also known as cookies.

Emma: True. Even cookies have limits. How R U?

Grace: Big fight w/ Shoshi.

Emma: Ruh-roh! 😲

Grace: OK now. Did your GG ever make cookies?

Emma: Not really.

Grace: 2 bad. GG's fav food?

Emma: 🍓

Grace: Ooo—lucky! K—gotta go. 👟👟

Emma: Lucky? 😕

Grace: BFN!

This exchange was so puzzling that I couldn't go back to triangles. What did Grace mean that strawberries are lucky? Why had she asked about GG and food?

Then there was the fight with Shoshi, who I remembered was her best school friend. I tried to think what I knew about Shoshi. She was smart. She was bossy. She was Jewish, like me. Before she and Grace became best friends, they had been worst enemies. I wondered what their fight was about anyway.

If Secret Cookie Club operations were on schedule, Lucy should have sent cookies to Grace by this time. And wait—hadn't Hannah's letter said that she'd sent cookies to Grace, too?

Maybe flour power had fixed the fight with Shoshi. It would be nice to think that was what happened.

CHAPTER FIFTEEN

Emma

Benjamin's scrimmage was down in Delaware, more than an hour away. At 6:16, my dad texted that the Junior Flyers had won 4–2, and he and Ben were about to get on the road to come home.

Woot! I texted back. See you soon!

I went to my door and looked down the hall. My parents' room is at the other end—beyond Ben's and Nathan's. I already mentioned Nathan—my brother who died before I was born. He was eight and got an infection. The doctors at the hospital couldn't stop it. There is no secret about this in my family, but it doesn't come up every day. Anyway, my parents' door was still closed, but I thought my mom would want to know about the Flyers. Maybe it would cheer her up.

"Mom?" I knocked softly. "Can I come in? *Mom?*"

The only answer was a little *unh* sound that I chose to translate as, *Sure, Emma! Come on in!*

I opened the door. My mom was sitting up in bed with a pile of pillows behind her. A little light came in from the window. The drapes were open, but it was dusk outside.

"Do you want me to turn on a light?" I asked.

"I'm fine," she said.

I sat down on the edge of the bed. "You don't look that fine. I could fix your hair if you want. Or you could come downstairs, and I could make you an egg. It isn't good to be up here all by yourself all day. You're practically in the dark! You would never let me or Ben get away with it."

This was not what I had intended to say. I had intended to deliver good news. But I was a tiny bit shocked by how crazy my mom's gray hair looked all splayed out on the pillow and by how pale her skin was. My mom may not have fashion sense, but she is always tidy.

"Don't boss me, Emma. I'm a grown woman. I will get up when I feel like it," Mom said.

"I'm not bossing you," I said.

"Yes, you are. Do you think it was the hair dye that killed her? It's not healthy. There are studies."

It was a second before I realized she was talking about GG, whose hair had been an unnatural shade of red ever since I could remember. I guessed it must've been dyed, but I had never thought about it.

"She was old, Mom. I think old was more the problem," I said.

"There was that woman on the news who was a hundred and ran a marathon," my mom said. "I bet *she* didn't dye her hair."

"Mom, are you okay?" I asked. "I don't think you're making sense."

"Remember how I said I'd be sad later?" she said. "Well, later has arrived, and I am too sad to make sense. Now, if you don't mind, I think I'll rest a little more."

"Okay." I stood up. "Uh . . . Ben won his scrimmage. That's what I came in to tell you. He and Dad are on their way home."

Mom closed her eyes. "Good."

"Are you coming down to eat with us?" I asked. "They'll be back in an hour or so, Dad said. I guess he's bringing dinner. Or should I heat up some soup?"

"Doesn't matter," Mom said.

"Are you going to work tomorrow?" I asked.

Mom opened her eyes. "Emma?"

"Sorry, Mom," I said. "I love you."

"I love you too," she said faintly.

When I went out, I closed the door without making any sound.

CHAPTER SIXTEEN

Emma

The next day Mom stayed home from work again. Just before seventh period, I got a text that my grandmother would pick me up. She drives a blue BMW with white leather seats that are so perfect I'm afraid to sit in them.

"Is Mom feeling better?" I asked as soon as I pulled the passenger door closed. "She never stays home from work."

My grandmother didn't answer immediately. She was busy maneuvering her big car in my school's small, busy parking lot. At last, she succeeded in turning left onto the street. "Hard to tell about your mom," she said. "What do you think, Emma? Has she been working especially hard?"

"I think she's sad about GG," I said.

"We are all sad about GG—about my mother," said Grandma. "I will always miss her, and I know you and your brother will as well. But, darling, the world keeps spinning, and there are things to do. We can't allow ourselves to fall apart."

"Now you sound like Mom," I said. "When something goes wrong, she encourages me to get past it."

We were stopped at a light. My grandma looked over and smiled. "Like mother, like daughter, I guess," she said.

"Do you think so?" I was surprised. My grandmother is thin with perfectly arched eyebrows. My mother is round and won't even wear lip gloss.

The light changed. "Both your mother and I have

strong opinions," said my grandmother. "Not that they're usually the same opinions. And both of us have confidence in ourselves. So yes, Emma"—she shrugged—"I'd say we are alike."

When there is no traffic, it's a twenty-minute ride from school to my house in Gladwyne. On the expressway Grandma and I talked about my classes and about Kayden, who is getting better at reading out loud even though he complains I make him work too hard. I gave her updates on my best friends, Caitlin and Julia.

But even while we were talking about other things, some part of my brain kept thinking of my mom. That's why, as we exited onto River Road, I said, "Grandma? Maybe you can figure out what's wrong with her—if you're so much alike, I mean. If it was you acting the way my mom is now, what would that mean was wrong with *you*?"

"Hang on." My grandmother watched a line of traffic pass, made a left turn, and checked her rearview mirror. "That's a hard one, Emma," she finally said.

"That is going to require some thinking."

When we got home, my grandmother announced she would stick around and fix dinner. She knows my parents usually grab pizza or a chicken or Chinese food from the supermarket. She thought a homemade meal would be a treat.

"Sure," I said, "but uh . . . what are you going to make, do you think? You probably know that Ben's kind of picky."

"It will be delicious," my grandmother said.

I checked on my mom, who seemed to be napping. Then I did my homework in my room. From the kitchen, I heard bumping and clanging. I smelled onions cooking with garlic and something suspiciously green. I hoped Ben would like it. I hoped if he didn't he wouldn't say anything bad. When my grandmother's offended, she gets frosty.

After my homework was done, I decided to e-mail Hannah. Usually my mom would have to bug me for a week to send a thank-you, but this time I guessed I was on my own.

Hey, Hannah, hi! How are you?

The lemon cookies were extremely delicious. Thank you! My little brother and my grandmother like them, and both of them are picky eaters.

I am sorry (I think?) about Jack. Is your heart broken? I can't tell from what you wrote. Someday I guess I will have a boyfriend, but I have never had one yet, and it seems to me like boys are a lot of trouble. For example, I think Vivek, not meaning to, caused trouble between Lucy and Grace. Like maybe Grace is jealous? But Lucy is her friend so she doesn't want to be jealous, and anyway Vivek and Grace broke up—right?—so Grace isn't really even allowed to be jealous.

I'm not sure that Lucy knows Vivek likes her. It is hard to tell with Lucy.

Do you think you and Jack will get back together?

Are you going to text Lance?

You don't have to tell me if you don't want to.

In my life everything is okay except my great-grand-mother died and my mom got sick. It is hard to tell if those two things are connected. I am a little worried about my mom, if you want to know the whole truth. Everyone misses GG, but my mom is the only one who won't come out of her room.

Thank you again very much for the cookies.

Your very favorite camper (ha-ha!), Emma

It was a little before six when I pressed send. At about the same time I heard my grandmother on the stairs. "Emma?" She appeared in my doorway. "Your dinner is all ready on the stove. You just have to warm it up, depending on when your dad and brother get home, I mean."

"Ben'll be dropped off soon. Dad won't be home till about seven," I said. "But where are you going?"

"Home," she said. "I'm not going to intrude on your evening."

"You can't intrude. You're family," I said.

"Thank you, honey, but we all have our weeknight routines. Oh, and I thought about what you asked before—what would be wrong with me if I were your mom?"

"So what do you think?" I asked.

Grandma smiled. "What I think is I need to think harder," she said. Her teeth are perfect too. "Up till now, I've always counted on GG for wisdom. Even if she was forgetful the last few years, she was still wise. I need to think about what *she* would have said, and maybe then it will come to me. Now come here and give me a hug."

Grandma's dinner turned out to be chicken with peas and potatoes. On the chicken were green specks, which Ben eyed suspiciously at first. Later he asked for seconds. For dessert, we ate lemon cookies.

Mom stayed upstairs, which—weirdly—was starting to seem normal. Dad, Ben, and I talked about all the usual stuff. We did not talk about Mom. It was like none of us wanted to say out loud that anything might be really wrong.

CHAPTER SEVENTEEN

Emma

Mom stayed in her room the rest of that week. My grandmother picked Ben and me up at school, made sure we got to hockey and tutoring and Hebrew school, organized dinner, and fed Ike.

On Friday afternoon, Ben finally broke the silence on Mom.

"Grandma, what's the matter with her?" he asked. We were sitting at the kitchen table. Grandma was making pasta sauce. She was in a hurry to get to some friends' house for Shabbat, the weekly dinner to welcome the Sabbath.

Grandma put a spoon in the sauce, tasted it, frowned, opened a cupboard, and got out the salt. "Your mother is sad and she can't get over it," she said. "Simple as that. She'll have to eventually, though. I, for one, am growing impatient."

Now I felt annoyed. My brother shouldn't have asked that question. My grandmother shouldn't have answered the way she did.

"Maybe she can't help it," I said. "Sometimes sadness becomes a disease called depression. We learned about it in health."

"I know all that," Grandma said. "I don't live in the Dark Ages, and I didn't say she could help it. I just said I'm impatient. Now"—Grandma spun around, checked her watch, and looked at me—"would you mind washing what's in the sink? It shouldn't go in the dishwasher. And, Benjamin, you set the table."

"I'm doing homework," I argued. "And how come Ben gets the easy job?"

Grandma's answer was to raise her eyebrows.

I didn't say anything. I got up to do the dishes. But I was growing impatient too. Having my grandmother in charge was a lot different from what I was used to. Kitchen cleanup is Benjamin's and my job, but my parents don't do much real cooking, so cleanup happens after dinner and fast.

Also, our parents are not nearly as bossy as my grandmother.

When the doorbell rang a few minutes later, I was scrubbing a pan. Benjamin—whose super-easy chore had taken about ten seconds—answered the door and brought back a package.

"I signed for it," he said.

"But it's my name on the label," I said.

"Will I get arrested?" Ben asked. "Maybe that would be okay. No more school, and I bet there's TV in jail."

Grandma frowned. "Bite your tongue, young man."

"Why?" Ben asked. "That would hurt."

"She means you shouldn't say you want to go to jail," I said. "Now, can I have my box, please?" The dishes by this time were done, and I had dried my hands. "Is it from Massachusetts? I think it's probably cookies."

"More cookies!" Grandma shook her head. "Now, Emma, not to be critical, but think before you eat too many."

"What's that supposed to mean?"

"Just a word to the wise," my grandmother said. "You know what studies say about sugar, not to mention gluten."

"There's glue in cookies?" Ben said.

"Glu-*ten*," I said. "No one knows what it is and everyone's afraid of it. I watched a video on YouTube."

"Gluten is a long-chain protein molecule found in grains like wheat," Grandma said. "It makes bread and other things chewy, and it's hard for some people to digest."

"Whoa, Grandma!" I was impressed.

"I told you I don't live in the Dark Ages," she said. "And I've got to be going, or I'll be late. Your dad should be here any minute. I love you two. You know that, right?"

"I know," Ben said.

"I guess," I said.

My grandmother looked at me. "Emma?"

"Oh, okay. I know too."

"Here's an idea," Grandma said. "What if some afternoon after school I take you shopping? You could use a new outfit for special occasions, don't you think?"

"Uh . . ." I thought fast. "That is a very kind and generous offer, but I am pretty busy after school."

"One of these days," Grandma said, "you and I will make time."

The cookies from Grace were the thumbprint kind with red jam in the center.

Probably raspberry, I thought. But just to be sure I took a bite, and guess what? Not raspberry at all but strawberry! Was it because strawberries were GG's favorite?

I rummaged around in the box and pulled out Grace's letter. It covered both sides of two sheets of white paper—four pages total. Grace had a lot to say!

Tuesday, Oct. 25

Dear Emma,

Flour power won't fix death, but I got an
idea when we were texting.

In the city my dad is from, Singapore,
they celebrate the Hungry Ghost Festival.
It is a little like Halloween (what are you
going as???), but it happens in late summer.
I think it would be acceptable to your GG's
ghost if you celebrate now. Chinese custom
says ghosts are hungry all the time, not just
during the festival.

What you do for the festival is two
things. First you burn money so that your
dead ancestors can buy everything they
need to be comfortable in the afterlife.
The second thing is you offer food for
the ghosts as a bribe so they don't haunt
you. (I think it is a very strange idea

that ghosts would want to haunt their own relatives. My dad thinks it is a very strange idea too.)

I asked about your great-grandmother's favorite food because it is especially good if that is what you put out as your offering. People in Singapore believe red is lucky, so it must be extra lucky that your great-grandmother liked a red food, strawberries.

I believe the combination of Hannah's grandpa's flour power and Chinese tradition will be very strong—strong enough (I hope!) to help your mother and you, too.

Now you are wondering: How are things in your life, Grace?

I will tell you.

Remember I said I had a fight with Shoshi?

What happened is because I messed up, her dog got sick, and I made things worse by fibbing about it because I was so embarrassed that I messed up. It was Lucy's idea for me confess because I would feel better, so I did, and instead I felt much worse because Shoshi got furious and told me to leave her house and did not want to be my friend anymore!

If that was the end of the story, the moral would be: Do not confess the truth.

But it is not the end of the story. The next day, Mr. Russen (social studies teacher) assigned a group project on an old temple on the Nile River. Shoshi likes to get the best grade in the class on everything, and she knew if her group was going to get the best grade, she needed me because I am best at writing. (She is best at drawing.)

I said okay, and then we had to work together, and I guess she realized (1) that even though I fibbed I am still nice, and (2) that I felt really, really bad about what happened when I messed up, and (3) it's true

I am good at group projects.

We got an A+.

Now we are friends again, so it turns out Lucy was right and you should tell the truth. After that, I confessed to my parents too, and they made me use my own saved-up money to pay back some people I never met for a carrot cake, which is a long story, and this letter is already long.

Also, Shoshi's dog got well just like I hope your mom will.

Also I made the Rubinsteins cookies and lemonade. I have to go to bed now because tomorrow I have to get up early for choir. Also, my hand is tired!

Good luck with the hungry ghost of GG.

Best from the best (ha-ha!), Grace Xi

P.S. My dad helped me bake these cookies. He says baking is going to be his hobby. He

is shopping for a fancy new oven for our
kitchen.

P.P.S. For Halloween, I am going as a
sugarplum fairy because I already have the
costume and, according to my parents, who
has time for one more thing?

My English teacher, Miss Conley, gives us a new
vocabulary word every Friday. This week's was *preposterous,* which means ridiculous, absurd, crazy—you get
the idea.

When I finished Grace's letter, *preposterous* was the
first word that came to mind. According to Miss Conley,
it comes from a Latin word that means last before first,
in other words, everything upside down and out of
order.

This perfectly described Grace's suggestion. Up till
now, I'd always thought she was one of my sensible
friends. Feeding a ghost was something Lucy or Olivia
would go for—like last summer at camp when Lucy

cast a spell over some cookies so that Lance, the cutest boy counselor, would fall in love with Hannah.

That hadn't exactly gone as planned. Why would this be any different?

I read the letter over and thought of something else. Was Grace saying my mom was tired all the time because the ghost of GG was haunting her?

CHAPTER EIGHTEEN

Emma

After services the next day, Saturday, I told Caitlin and Julia about Grace's letter. It was a warm day for October. We were sitting in the sun on a bench in the courtyard at the temple, drinking red punch and chewing ice.

"I get it," said Caitlin. "It's like an exorcism in a scary movie when you make the ghost leave."

Julia shook her head. "Feeding the ghost is totally different."

I asked Julia how she knew that, which was dumb of me. Julia knows everything.

"I did a report in second grade," she said. "Supposedly ghosts are irritable all the time because they don't like being dead."

"Did you say 'irritable' in your report in second grade?" Caitlin asked.

"My mom helped me write it," Julia said. "I think a cookie offering is a good idea, Emma."

"I agree," said Caitlin. "Plus it's so close to Halloween, the ghosts will come out for sure."

"Are you guys serious?" I said. "The whole thing is preposterous."

"No, it's not. It's a ritual," Julia said, "like Sabbath candles or a Christmas tree. Like saluting the flag."

"Or burying your pet rat when it dies," said Caitlin, "and marking its grave with sticks and shiny pebbles."

"Are you comparing my great-grandmother to a dead rat?" I asked.

"I loved my rat," said Caitlin.

"Chinese culture is old," said Julia, "even older than Jewish culture. It stands to reason by now the Chinese know something."

"Do you remember from your report what we're supposed to do exactly?" I asked.

"I think you need incense," said Julia.

"Strawberry incense," said Caitlin, "since that's what your GG liked."

"And money that you can burn," said Julia. "But it can be pretend. The ghosts don't care."

"Oh, yeah, right," I said. "Everybody knows *that* about ghosts. I think you're both crazy, and Grace too."

"Maybe." Julia shrugged.

"But if you decide you do want to try it," Caitlin said, "we will definitely come over and help. You said Grace sent jam cookies, right? I remember those cookies she sent last year. I bet these are really good."

The next day was Sunday—the two-week anniversary of the day that GG died. Nothing had been normal around my house since.

Was that how it always was when somebody died?

When would I get my mom back?

When Dad came downstairs, I asked him how she was doing, and he shrugged. "About the same. She says she might come down later."

"She said that yesterday, but she didn't," I said.

"I know that, Emma," my dad said.

"So when is she going to? Why can't you do something? You're a doctor! Isn't there a pill or a shot that will make her better?"

My dad slumped down in his chair. "There are medications for depression," he said, "but she should talk to a specialist first, and she says she doesn't need to."

For the past few days a question had been nagging me. The subject was something we didn't talk about a lot in my family, but now it seemed like we had to. "Dad, was Mom like this after Nathan died?"

I had thought my dad would look surprised, but he didn't. Maybe he had been thinking back to that time too. "She wasn't," he said. "I was the one who fell apart while she made all the arrangements. She even cooked for the guests while we sat shivah. Then she went back to work. She never missed a beat."

"Did you talk about it?" I asked.

"We talked a lot about how much we missed him," he said. "It's just our reactions were different. Remember what I said about grieving on your own schedule? That's why."

Now my dad shrugged and squeezed his eyes shut like they hurt. Suddenly, I felt bad. My parents are older than most of my friends' parents. I don't think about it often, but looking at my dad right then I did.

I told my dad about the hungry ghost ceremony after breakfast. I was hoping to make him smile. We were in the family room. It has a lot of windows and looks out on our backyard, which is more like a back forest. The trees were black and shiny bare. Their fallen leaves formed a bright-colored carpet on the ground.

My dad did smile, and then he surprised me. "Why not try it?" he said. "GG loved her sweets—especially anything strawberry. She would have gotten a kick out of the whole thing."

"Oh, come on, Dad. You don't believe in ghosts or haunting," I said. "It's totally unscientific."

"Totally," Dad agreed. "But you know what they say, Emma. There are more things in heaven and earth than are dreamt of in your philosophy."

"I didn't know they said that," I said. "And who are *they* anyway?"

"It's a quotation from Shakespeare," Dad said, "from the play called *Hamlet*. The idea is no matter how hard we study and how scientific we are, there will always be mysteries. So when are you planning to get busy and appease the ghosts?"

"Uh . . . I guess that depends on what 'appease' means," I said.

"Make them feel better," said Dad. "In other words, have the ceremony. The weather's pretty brisk today—a good time for someone to do some baking."

Suddenly things started to make sense. "Someone?" I repeated. "Do you mean me? Is this really about cookies? I'm not supposed to bake more, you know. Grace wants us to use the ones she sent. That's why she made them with strawberry jam."

"I have bad news regarding those cookies, Em," Dad said. "They are, uh, basically . . . all gone."

"Basically?" I said.

"Totally," he clarified.

"How did that happen?" I asked.

"One at a time?" he said.

"*Da-a-ad!* Haven't you ever heard of emotional intelligence?"

"Sure," Dad said, "and that's just what this was. I had a long, boring paper to read, and I bribed myself with cookies. If that's not intelligent, I don't know what is. Tell you what: I'll make a supermarket run. You just tell me what you need. Strawberry jam, right?"

"And incense," I said. If everyone was determined to feed the ghost, I might as well go along.

CHAPTER NINETEEN

Emma

I made Dad a list and sent him to the store. Then, because sunset seemed like a good time for a ghost ceremony, I looked up when it was that day—6:06 p.m.— and sent an e-vite to Caitlin and Julia. After that, I found my brother playing video games in the basement, sat down on the arm of the nearest sofa, and explained to him what we were doing.

"Ghosts *and* cookies?" He looked up from the controller. "That's as good as Halloween monsters and candy."

"We're not doing this for fun," I said. "We're doing it to make Mom feel better."

"Makes sense," he said. *"Not."*

"I don't get how it's supposed to work either," I said. "But other people seem to think it might."

"If it's because GG really is haunting Mom," Ben said slowly, "then I wish she'd haunt me instead. Or—I know—maybe if she wants to haunt somebody *new*, I could make suggestions. Are we inviting Grandma?"

"I didn't think of it," I said. "What do you think?"

"I'm not sure Grandma will understand."

"Me neither," I said. "What if we tell her all about it after?"

"Like when Mom feels better," Ben said. "Can I help?"

Whoa—maybe this feed-the-ghost thing *was* magic. My little brother was offering to help!

"You can find the old Monopoly game," I told him. "We need some play money out of it."

"Are you sure that's okay?" Ben frowned. "Monopoly was Nathan's, wasn't it?"

"Just get a few dollars," I said. "We'll still be able to play."

"Hey," Ben said. "Did you think of this? Maybe Nathan's ghost is hungry too."

I felt something strange when Ben said that. It was like a twinge in my heart. Till now I'd been thinking of GG, the happy ghost of a happy old lady who had lived a long life. Thinking of Nathan was different. His death had been a tragedy. He was a kid—a year younger than Ben is now. Unlike GG, he couldn't possibly have been ready for whatever came next. How could he be a happy ghost?

Ben must have felt the same twinge I did. "Never mind," he said. "I'll go get the game."

"I think Dad's back." I stood up. "I better start baking."

"Do we eat cookies too, or only the ghosts get to?" Ben asked.

"Depends on how hungry they are," I said.

* * *

Baking and preparing for the ceremony kept me busy the rest of that day. Even if the whole thing was preposterous, I liked that I was doing something to move things back to normal.

The setup was complete by five fifteen. Only then did I think of my mom. I mean, since the point of the ceremony was to make her better, I'd been thinking of her all day. At the same time, I'd been so busy I hadn't actually gone to see her, let alone ask her to come downstairs.

I could've gone to her bedroom right then, but something held me back. I guess I was afraid she'd say no, or even get mad.

Pondering this, my mind made a turn and asked an easier question. What was the dress code for a hungry ghost ceremony?

Grace would know that one, so I texted her. The answer came back: Normal clothes. Say ♡ to GG.

Normal clothes?

Boring!

I put Mom off again and went up to my room. On my laptop, I brought up the photos I had found when

I'd searched how to do the ceremony. Most of them showed men wearing what looked like orange sheets. The captions explained that the men were Buddhist monks. I didn't have an orange sheet, but I had an old orange nightgown—and guess what? It was a present from GG!

I found it in my bottom drawer, shook out the wrinkles, and held it up to check the length. I guessed I had grown some; it was a little short. Still, I had to wear it. What would be better for a hungry ghost ceremony honoring GG?

The doorbell rang while I was fixing my hair. On the porch were Caitlin and Julia, right on time. Each of them held a pizza.

"OMG, what are you *wearing?*" asked Caitlin as they followed me into the house. They were wearing normal jeans and T-shirts.

"It's what you're supposed to wear to this kind of a ceremony," I said. "Only I forgot to put it on the e-vite. How come you brought pizza?"

"Dad drove us, and he made us get it," said Julia. "He

said the ghosts deserved more than cookies. He thinks he is hilarious."

"They're both just plain cheese," Caitlin said. "We didn't know how ghosts felt about toppings."

Even still in boxes, the pizza smelled delicious, and I realized I was hungry for something besides cookies and cookie dough. At the same time, I was annoyed. Who ever heard of pizza at a hungry ghost ceremony?

In the kitchen, Ike had smelled the pizza too. As he made his way out from under the table, he wagged not only his tail but his whole rear end. His head was bowed in gratitude to any human that just might give him a bite.

"Good dog, Ike," said Julia. "You want some pizza, don't you?"

"Ghosts do not like pizza, only cookies," I said.

"How do you know that?" Caitlin asked.

"Research," I said.

"You are making it up," Caitlin said.

"What if she is? We can eat the pizza after," said Julia.

By this time it was almost sunset and the mom

question had to be dealt with. How I did it was I went to find my brother and I told him to bring her down.

"Tell her there's a ghost ceremony. Tell her she needs to be here," I said.

"No way." Ben shook his head. "She will think I'm crazy."

"Then skip the ghost part, and tell her to come to the dining room," I said.

"I'll get Dad to." Ben headed down the hall.

"Hurry!" I said.

CHAPTER TWENTY

Emma

We have a pretty big house, I guess, and a pretty big dining room, too. My dad jokes that he can't see my mom
when they are at opposite ends of the table. Twice a
year on holidays, my mom announces we are getting
rid of the striped wallpaper that was here when they
moved in. But we never do.

I had laid an old linen cloth on the table. On top of
it I had placed three sticks of incense in a crystal bud

vase, a neat and symmetrical pile of perfect (if I do say so myself) strawberry thumbprint cookies on a china dinner plate, and half a dozen pink Monopoly dollars on a china salad plate. Caitlin, Julia, and I stood around the table, waiting for everybody else. I lit the incense. Two breaths later, the sweet, burned smell overwhelmed my nose.

"Is that strawberry?" Caitlin asked.

"Cherry spice," I said. "The closest my dad could find."

A moment later Dad and Ben came in, but there was still no Mom.

"Is she coming down?" I asked.

"She says she's too tired. I tried," said Dad.

"Will it work if she doesn't?" Caitlin asked.

"I was afraid this might happen," I said, "so I texted Grace yesterday. She said as long as we're all in the same house, it ought to work. Is everybody ready? First we burn the money."

"Is that a good idea?" Dad asked.

"We have adult supervision," I said.

"You mean me," Dad said.

"Get a glass of water," I told Ben.

"Bossy," said Ben.

"Please," I said.

Ben turned around and went for water.

"We should turn out the lights," said Julia.

"Who put you in charge?" said Caitlin.

"Hello-o-o? I wrote the report!" said Julia.

"In second grade," muttered Caitlin.

Ben came back with the water. Julia turned out the lights. The room turned shadowy-gloomy but not entirely dark. Carefully, I struck a match and touched the flame to a Monopoly dollar. Its corner turned black, then curled. I was afraid it might wilt instead of burning, then—*poof*—the scraps blazed brilliant yellow before fading in a moment to sorrowful smoke and ash.

A poetical person like Lucy would have seen the burst of light and thought how our lives on earth are short. I saw it and worried the fire might leave a spot on the plate.

"Now do we say words or something?" Caitlin asked.

"We should say words in Chinese," Ben said.

"I can say 'hello' and 'thank you' in both Cantonese and Mandarin," said Julia.

"Those aren't the words we want," I said. "I didn't find anything good online, but what matters is that we remember GG. And all the other ghosts too. In the afterlife—in heaven—we wish you every comfort."

"And cookies!" said Benjamin.

"And cookies!" said Dad and Caitlin and Julia.

In my imagination I saw GG as clearly as if she were in the room with us. She was clapping her hands and smiling her awesome smile. After that I seemed to hear her voice: *All this for one old lady? Boy, did I ever luck out in the family department!*

Ben said, "It's not only for you. It's for Nathan, too."

Wait. Who was Ben talking to? I looked over at him. "What did you—"

"Nothing," Ben said quickly. "Nobody." But his eyes were wide like he'd seen a you-know-what. Had something strange just happened?

"Who's Nathan?" Caitlin asked, and then she must've remembered because she said, "Oh!" and

"Sorry," and covered her mouth with her hand.

"It's okay, Caitlin," my dad said. "Ben and Emma's brother died before you were born."

I was still trying to figure out Ben's comment when I heard a noise upstairs. Was it a ghost? And then the doorbell rang.

Ben said, "I'll get it." He left the room and returned a minute later. Behind him was Grandma.

"What are you doing here?" I asked. Then I realized how that sounded and added, "Uh, great to see you."

Grandma said, "I was in the neighborhood." Then she surveyed the room, inhaled some incense, and wrinkled her nose. "What's going on here exactly? What's that I smell? Emma, your brother said you would explain."

Julia spoke before I had the chance. "We're appeasing hungry ghosts."

"Nice word usage," said Dad.

Grandma shook her head. "Do you mean Halloween? Isn't it early for that? What's that you're wearing, Emma? Is this some kind of a slumber party?"

"That's a lot of questions," said Ben.

"I have a few myself." Mom appeared in the doorway behind them. She looked, I have to say, kind of witchy. Her wild gray hair had not calmed down since Sunday. She wore a black bathrobe and her pj's.

"Why don't we sort this out over pizza?" Dad said. "I may not be a ghost, but I am hungry."

It took about five minutes to move the ceremony stuff to the sideboard and bring in pizza, plates, napkins, and glasses from the kitchen. We sat around one end of the big, formal table, with Grandma at the head. With a lot of help from Julia, I explained. I left out the part about GG haunting my mom. I just said the ceremony was Chinese and for GG, and besides, we had run out of cookies so I baked some.

"It all sounds, if you'll forgive me, quite preposterous," said Grandma, who was taking delicate bites of pizza, cut with knife and fork.

"That's why we didn't tell you," Ben said. He was chewing as he spoke.

"Ben!" I said.

"What?" He swallowed. "It doesn't mean we don't love her."

Someone giggled. I looked around and I saw that it was Mom. "Sorry," she said. "Of course we love you, Mother."

"Are you feeling better, dear?" my grandmother asked her. "Do you think perhaps you'll be able to return to your usual schedule tomorrow?"

"No need to if you're not up to it," my dad said quickly. I think he was annoyed with Grandma.

My mother said, "I'm still pretty tired," and then changed the subject. "Did anyone see any ghosts?"

"Not me," said Caitlin, "unfortunately." And all of us shook our heads—Benjamin too.

"We don't really believe in them," I said.

"They're supposed to be cranky," said Caitlin, "irritable, I mean."

"I bet they're lonely," Mom said. "I bet they're afraid they'll be forgotten. I bet they miss what they've left behind."

"Do *you* believe in ghosts, Mom?" Ben asked.

"Not the spooky kind that float around making trouble," Mom said, "but there are ghosts that live in our minds, the memories of loved ones who died."

I said, "Like Nathan," and instantly felt bad. The words had just popped out.

Mom didn't seem to mind, though. In fact, she looked better—more awake and more herself—than she had in a while. "I miss him every day," she said.

"Me too," Dad said. "He'd be twenty-one now. He'd probably be in college."

"He would like having a little brother," said Ben.

"And a little sister," I said.

"I bet he's with GG," said Ben. "They're keeping each other company."

My dad said that was a nice thought, and my mom reached over and squeezed Ben's shoulder. Then my grandmother did something that for her was shocking: My grandmother started to cry!

Her tears threw us all into a tizzy. My mom got up for tissues. My dad got up for a glass of water. Caitlin just stared until Julia kicked her, and then they both got up to clear the table.

Ben and I helped.

Once the tears were over, the apologies began—first my grandmother for her tears and then Ben for making her cry.

"You didn't do anything wrong," Grandma reassured him. "It *was* a nice thought—the two of them together. I can't think why it set me off like that."

"I think I know," Mom said. "You've tried to postpone being sad, same as I did. In the end, though, it turns out the ghosts won't let you get away with it."

"Like mother, like daughter," my grandmother said.

"Could be," said my mother. "And now do you know what we need?"

"Cookies?" I suggested.

"Exactly right," said my mother. "We've given the ghosts a fair chance to eat them. What they've left must be for the rest of us."

We were back in the dining room by this time, sitting

around the table again. I pushed my chair back and went over to the sideboard. The bud vase was there with the burned incense sticks. The china salad plate was there with the ashy remains of Monopoly money. The china dinner plate was there too . . . and it was empty. The thumbprint cookies had disappeared.

CHAPTER TWENTY-ONE

Monday, January 15, Olivia

I love love, love, love, *love* Christmas, and in our family, it's a very big deal.

Too big, according to Jenny and Ralph, who *tsk-tsk* and shake their heads every time the subject comes up.

Jenny and Ralph—if you're wondering—live with my family in an apartment downstairs in our house. Since before I was born, their job has been to help take care of us. My parents value Jenny and Ralph's opinion, and every year right after Thanksgiving they agree that Jenny and Ralph are entirely right and they will turn down the volume because the last thing this family needs is more *stuff.*

Jenny nods approvingly when my parents say this. Ralph winks and gives them a big thumbs-up.

Then my parents go right out and buy as much as they did the year before, and they have all of it wrapped and placed under the tall and super-ginormous tree the gardener sets up in the living room.

Not that I'm complaining. I happen to like all the silver-gold-twinkly Christmas decorations, not to mention the prezzies—especially the ones marked FOR OLIVIA, FROM SANTA because they don't require thank-you notes.

Secretly, I think Jenny and Ralph must like Christmas too. For example, Ralph gets to spend a whole day with Jenny by the tree while she gives him the very best advice on precisely where every light and ornament ought to go. Then he gets to spend two whole days hanging lights outside and several hours hanging wreaths and garlands and other decorations on banisters and over doorways throughout the house.

Meanwhile, Jenny makes about a million Christmas cookies for my parents to give away to the people who work at our family's business, Baron Barbecue Sauce. Maybe you've heard of it. Maybe you have a bottle in your refrigerator right now. If you do, you can go take a look at my parents; that's their picture on the label. Sometimes I think this is embarrassing, and sometimes I think at least we don't make dog food.

Being eleven years old, I have seen my fair share of Christmases, and I know a thing or two about the way they come and go. The going part—the so very, very sad, sad, sad, *sad* part—happens in stages. First the boxes and wrapping paper are recycled, second the presents are put away, and third the leftovers are eaten.

This year the final stages happened over the weekend. On Saturday, the gardener wrestled the tree out of the house—leaving needles everywhere—then he hauled it away to be chipped into mulch. Jenny, meanwhile, vacuumed. After that, she and I packed the ornaments back in their boxes and the boxes back in their storage room on the third floor.

I helped even though I didn't have to and even without being asked because I am a good and generous young person and also because of the little incident in the kitchen on Friday when, while demonstrating a perfect handstand, I miscalculated my left foot's return to the floor, kicked the kitchen table (*ow!*), and broke Jenny's favorite teacup.

"Sorry," I said, rubbing my poor, sad, bruised toes.

Jenny placed her hands on her hips and stared down at the pieces.

"What if you look on the bright side?" I tried. "Now I know what to get you for your birthday."

"The teacup was my mother's," Jenny said. Then she raised her face and looked at me with narrowed eyes.

"Really, really very, very, *very* sorry," I said.

"And?" said Jenny.

"And . . . uh, I'll sweep that up for you?" I said.

"You do that, please," said Jenny.

"Right away," I said, and then I did, and then I helped with the ornaments, too.

On Monday, with Christmas well and truly gone,

Hannah's utterly scrumptious lemon cookies arrived to make me feel better. You might consider this *ironic*—which means an upside-down coincidence—because Hannah is Jewish and doesn't even celebrate Christmas. I, instead, considered it further evidence that the universe is on my side and wants to help me get through even the darkest days.

What can I say? I am lucky like that is all.

After school that day I had come up the steps to the front door and seen that the wreath was gone and felt a stabbing sadness in my heart: Christmas was over! How would I survive the long, dark, lonely winter?

In the living room, I took a picture of the bare space where the tree had been and posted it with an emoji of a crying polar bear wearing a Santa hat. Then I hop-scotched across the black-and-white marble squares in the foyer and walked through the dining room to the kitchen to find Jenny and see what there was for snack. Right there on the counter was the box addressed to me, Olivia Baron, in Kansas City, MO. The return address was Floral Park, NY.

I knew right away what was in that box: cookies from Hannah!

(She is my only friend in Floral Park.)

Jenny was busy with bowls and knives and vegetables—organizing dinner. She said hello and asked me something about the box. To be honest, I wasn't totally listening. My friend Dominique had sent me an Instagram of a slice of pizza that was purple, and I was trying to figure out if it was beets or a filter or what, and besides that the likes had started to come in for my polar-bear-Christmas post—twelve so far.

"Olivia!" Jenny said. "Hello?"

"Hello, Jenny," I said. "How are you this sad, sad afternoon? At least"—I sighed sorrowfully—"there are cookies to provide solace. May I have a knife?"

"I'll open the box for you, sweetheart," Jenny said. "Cookies, is it? Now, who are they from again?"

I started to tell her about Hannah, my counselor for two summers at Moonlight Ranch, and about the Secret Cookie Club, but my phone kept buzzing with likes, and Dominique was posting more rainbow pictures of pizza. What was up with that, anyway?

"Olivia?" Jenny said.

"Oh, you opened the box. Thank you," I said. The kitchen had filled with the summery sweet smell of lemonade. "*Yum*—have a cookie, Jenny. May I have a glass of milk? Hey, look at this. I wouldn't eat pink pizza, would you?"

"Probably not," said Jenny, "and I'll pass on the cookies, too, even though they do smell wonderful." She patted her tummy as if she were fat, which she isn't. "Now, look here, there's a letter in the box. Here you go, Olivia. Olivia?"

"Unh-hunh," I said. Esmee Snyder had just posted that video of the cat and the mirror—I mean, *who* hasn't seen that one at least a thousand times?

"Olivia!" Jenny said again.

"Unh-hunh," I said. "Oh—thanks for the milk. These cookies are delicious. You should have some. Hannah made them. Did I say that already?"

Jenny sighed and shook her head. "Talking to you is a misery, Olivia. You know that, right?"

"No, I don't," I said, "and furthermore"—I clapped my hand to my chest—"I am mortally wounded that you hold that opinion. OMG, Richard, the cute boy from math, hearted my taco-chip post from lunch. I think I might be in love!"

Jenny sighed. "That's nice. I think I might make dinner."

I looked up from my phone. "Wait," I said. "Don't you want to know about school? And I was going to tell you about Hannah and the cookie club, too—or did I already?"

I had always thought of Jenny as a very patient person, but that afternoon she got a little snippy, which is Mom language for not cranky yet but definitely on that road.

"Maybe you could put your phone down for a few moments, and we'll talk," Jenny said.

"Sure," I said, "of course," and I was about to, except first I had to post a picture of Hannah's cookies, and then I thought I better take another one of me eating Hannah's cookies, but the lighting was bad and my nose looked shiny. So I had to fix that and add some blue hair highlights too.

I tried to show Jenny the photo after I posted it, but she was peeling carrots and barely paid attention. "I prefer the real you to the you on a screen," she said. Now, what was that supposed to mean?

CHAPTER TWENTY-TWO

Olivia

After snack, I took Hannah's letter upstairs to my room and made myself comfortable among the pillows, power cords, and stuffed animals on my bed. I opened the envelope with my name on it and pulled out one sheet of paper. Hannah hadn't written much, I noticed.

I checked my phone one more time. The polar-bear-Christmas picture had fifty-two likes and six comments, none of them from Richard.

He hadn't liked the cookie pictures, either.

Obviously, something was wrong with me. Since when was I unpopular? Since when was I unloved?

I inhaled deeply for strength. Then I started to read.

Thursday, January 11

Hey there, Olivia!

Quick note because I don't have much time. Travis is picking me up, and we are going to the movies. It's his turn to choose, so there will be car chases, laser weapons, guys acting gross, or all three. It turns out the patience I learned being a counselor at Moonlight Ranch comes in handy the rest of the year. ☺

Here the weather is freezing and I am a little bored because spring semester classes haven't started. I am looking forward to learning more about Renaissance painting. When I was your age, I probably would have thought that sounded boring, but they make school more interesting when you're older.

These lemon cookies were baked this morning. My recipe is on the way to becoming world famous, if I do say so myself. My grandfather, the baker, would be proud. Travis loves it when I bake, so I am saving him a few.

Do you remember me talking about Travis? He's the guy I was seeing right before camp started last summer, and then we had a misunderstanding, and now—since Thanksgiving—we are back together. He goes to the same college I do, so I am super happy.

How are you? How was your Christmas? How is your beautiful family? Is your brother playing baseball this year? I know it's hard, but try to be patient about that. I bet secretly he appreciates having you at his games.

Gotta go. Travis can't stand being late to the movies. One time he turned right around and walked out!
Happy New Year, O, and enjoy the cookies!

Your one and only Flowerpot counselor, Hannah

P.S. I am already getting letters about this summer from Paula in the Moonlight Ranch office. Can't wait to see you then!

At least someone *is popular and loved,* I thought when I looked up from Hannah's letter. Not like yours truly. Oh, sure, I've had plenty of boyfriends, but none as good as Richard, who never volunteers to do the problems on the board but gets them right if he's called on. Plus I like his blond curly hair and the way his forehead wrinkles when he's thinking.

By this time entire minutes had passed with no news from my phone. I was about to check it but leaned back against my pillows for a second and closed my eyes. Instantly, a picture of Flowerpot Cabin popped into my head—the four of us campers sitting on the smooth clay floor with Hannah, working on a flag to represent us in the mess hall.

After that a slide show of pictures went by: Grace storming out of the dining hall when I teased her about Vivek, my horse Shorty alongside the beautiful bay show horse Brianna Silverbug had brought from home, me playing lookout while Lucy, Grace, and Emma studied the breakup letter from Travis that Hannah had thrown away.

Hey, wait.

I opened my eyes.

Travis?

Hannah's letter was still in my lap. I read it again and—*holy Christmas!*—she was back with that same guy, the one who dumped her! The one we had all agreed was a loser!

What had happened to the other one, the nice one, the counselor from whatzit cabin who was so funny and wore that old-man hat?

Jack—that was his name. Jack.

Emma would know what had happened. Right? Or Grace would. I sat up straight and grabbed my phone, ready to text, but I never even typed an emoji.

"Olivia!" my mother called up the stairs. "Dinner!"

CHAPTER TWENTY-THREE

Olivia

One day you will hear that a smart, fashionable, well-spoken African-American girl with an exceptional singing voice has run away from her home in Kansas City, Missouri, and that girl will be me.

Why?

Because my parents don't allow phones at the table.

You will probably want to read that again because you didn't believe it the first time.

Talk about missing out! Half my friends could be taken by zombies in the time it takes my family to eat, and I would never know. As it is, they regularly live a miniseries worth of drama, and when I find out it's too late to catch up.

Here's another thing: My parents are hypocrites! According to them, it's 100 percent okay to read the newspaper at breakfast.

Excuse me? How is the newspaper different from a phone?

"No batteries," says my brother, who thinks he is a laugh riot. Besides, whose side is he on, anyway? Isn't he a kid too? Shouldn't the kids stick together on matters of vital importance?

We eat dinner in the dining room every night because, my parents say, it's wasteful to have a room we don't use. There is always a clean cloth on the table and napkins to match. In the center is an old silver bowl with an arrangement of flowers, either from the garden or the florist. Today it was blue hydrangeas.

My mother had us on a healthy-eating kick, and that

night's healthy-eating creation was a Chinese stir-fry with shrimp.

My father scrutinized the plate after Jenny set it before him. "There seem to be bugs in my food," he said.

Jenny frowned. "Very funny, Mr. Baron."

"You know very well I'm kidding," my father said. "I have the highest regard for your abilities in the kitchen."

"Mm-*hm*," said Jenny. Then she served my brother and finally me before returning to the kitchen.

"Bugs and shrimp are closely related biologically," my brother said. His name is Troy. He's a senior in high school. He plays baseball. My parents love him best. "They both have exoskeletons. Mammals like us have endoskeletons."

"Everyone knows that," I said.

"But we don't have to discuss it at the dinner table," my mother said. "Now, whose turn is it to give thanks?"

"Troy's," I said.

"Livia's," Troy said at the same time.

My mother shook her head and looked at me. "Olivia? Why don't you do the honors tonight?"

See what I mean that they love Troy best?

"Heavenly father," I began, "thank you for this house and for this meal. Thank you for most of this family. Thank you for inventing the iPhone. Thank you for my good friend Hannah who sent me cookies today, which, if my family shows sufficient appreciation, I may deign to share for dessert tonight. Amen."

I swear I hadn't even opened my eyes yet when Troy attacked. "Did you really just thank God for inventing the iPhone? Do you know how stupid you sound?"

"*Troy*," said my father.

"Well, she does sound stupid," Troy said. "Steve Jobs invented the iPhone. Everyone knows that. There's even a movie."

"At church they say nothing happens without God," I said. "So that includes phones. Anyway, isn't Steve Jobs dead?"

"What's curious to me is that you think about your phone when you're saying grace," my father said.

"She's always thinking about her phone," said my brother.

I said, "That's not true!" and it wasn't. At that moment I'd been thinking about whether Richard had liked my polar bear post yet. If not, it must mean he didn't like me but only my taco chips.

"This argument is unlikely to be productive," said my mother. "So how 'bout if we cool it, okay?"

I nodded and grumbled and took a bite. Troy did the same. I must be growing again because even after cookies I was hungry—too hungry to let the close family ties between shrimp and bugs disturb me in any way.

For a few minutes we talked about school and which football teams would win the playoffs and go to the Super Bowl. Mrs. Wanderling, my after-school drama studio teacher, was getting ready to announce her choice for the spring play, and my mom and I speculated on what it would be and who (me!) would play the lead.

It was all very mannerly and polite, the way my parents require meals to be. Having eaten this way all my life, I don't think about it much, but my friends tell me when they come to dinner they are nervous wrecks worrying they'll interrupt somebody or chew with their mouths open.

Finished eating, my mother rang the silver bell that sits beside her wineglass, and Jenny came in to clear the plates. "How did you like the stir-fry?" she asked.

"Excellent," said my mother. "How many servings of vegetables did you say are in it?"

"Recipe says you each got two," Jenny said.

"Rabbit food," my father mumbled, which made my brother laugh.

"You'll thank me when you're old and healthy," my mother told him.

"I'm old *now*," said my father. "What's for dessert?"

"You'll see," Jenny said. Then she winked at me and I winked back. Soon she was bringing out Hannah's cookies on a tray along with glasses of milk for Troy and me, decaf for my mom and tea for my dad.

"They smell divine," my mother said, "but what's in them? Not too much butter, I hope."

"Probably full of vegetables," my father said. "Now, quick, grab your allotment before I finish them all."

For a few moments, we all enjoyed cookies. Then my mother mentioned that she and her assistant had gone over options for our family's spring vacation that afternoon.

"It would be wonderful, Troy," Mom said, "if you could join us for a day or two, depending on baseball, I mean. I was thinking the Canadian Rockies. Even if it's another warm winter, we ought to be able to ski there."

Troy shrugged. "I'm down."

"Has your coach announced the schedule yet?" my dad asked.

"I don't know," Troy said, "but it doesn't make any difference. I'm not playing baseball this year."

CHAPTER TWENTY-FOUR

Olivia

Ordinarily, I don't pay much attention to my brother when he talks, but I heard that. In fact, the bite of cookie in my mouth dissolved because I forgot to chew.

As for my parents, they froze.

Troy, meanwhile, finished his cookie. "Really good, Livia," he said. "Which one of your friends sent them again?"

I stammered something about Hannah and who she

was. Then, because my parents still looked incapable of speech, I kept right on talking: "Hannah made cookies like these for Grace and Emma, too. Did you know she broke up with Jack? At least, I guess she must've because now she's seeing Travis. Travis hates to be late to movies. I think that might mean he's bossy, don't you?"

No one answered me (*surprise!*), but by then my father's voice had returned. "We will discuss this, Troy," he said, "after I've put my thoughts together."

Troy shrugged with one shoulder. "Nothing to discuss," he said. "It's done."

"But baseball has been so important to you." My mother's voice was unnaturally sweet. "You've devoted so many hours."

"Enough hours," Troy said. "And now no more. I've got better things to do."

"Such as?" said my father.

"Vacation with my family," Troy said.

"That part will be nice," my mother said.

"No, it won't," said my father, "because it isn't happening."

"Uh, excuse me?" said Troy. "It's my life, Dad."

My father ignored this and looked at my mother. "Why didn't Coach Droske call me?"

"George," said my mother, "Troy is right. It's his decision."

"It's a bad decision," said my father, "and a parent's role is to steer his children away from bad decisions."

Up until this point, Troy had stayed really calm—unnaturally calm, come to think about it. But now his frustration came out. "I hate it when you act like you know everything," he told my dad.

My dad kept his voice even. "I would never make that claim," he said. "But I've been hanging 'round the planet for thirty years more than you, and I've kept my eyes open. I have a pretty good idea what leads to success and what doesn't. This is why, when you think of it, God put grown-ups in charge of kids, young man, and not the other way around."

Uh-oh. When my dad says "young man" that way, there is bound to be trouble. I, Olivia Baron, did not want to stick around to see it.

"I have homework," I announced, and stood up so quickly I almost knocked my chair over.

No one bothered to look.

"Hello-o-o?" I said. "Good-bye? Effective immediately, I am excusing myself and departing the dining room. You are all very welcome for the cookies."

Strangely, no one protested my leaving—even though I made more noise than necessary marching across the floor. Back upstairs, I threw myself across my bed, stared at the pink stars on my ceiling, and thought: *I should be shouting for joy.*

Ever since I was a baby in a stroller, I had been forced against my will to go to baseball games. Now, at long last, I wouldn't have to. No more extra innings on hard bleachers in the freezing-cold spring! No more scoreless ties on splintery bleachers in the hot, sweaty summer!

But I wasn't shouting for joy, and here's why: There were good parts to baseball, too. My brother's teammates, some of them extremely adorably super cute, were almost always nice to his kid sister, also known as *me.* Also, my parents, usually so particular about what

I eat and how I eat it, loosened up at games, where I was allowed to buy my own hot dogs, chips, sodas, and ice cream bars from the concession stand and eat them standing up with no napkin if I wanted.

Besides—and swear you'll never tell anyone—it was exciting anytime someone on my brother's team made a good play, even when the someone was my spoiled, stuck-up brother himself.

Trying to sort out my random and conflicting thoughts was very, very hard work. For a break, I grabbed my phone, and—*yes!* Richard had reacted with a sad face to my crying polar bear in a Santa hat!

What did that mean, exactly? Like me, was he sad that Christmas was over? Or (even better!) was he sad that I was sad?

Never mind my stupid brother and his stupid baseball drama.

This was important.

CHAPTER TWENTY-FIVE

Olivia

My brother's announcement would mean changes for my family and for my brother especially. But the next morning I found out that one thing wouldn't change: Troy's daily smoothie.

A couple of years ago Troy's coach had brought in a nutrition guy to talk to the players. This guy believed in protein shakes, and soon everyone on the team was drinking them for breakfast. Since Troy hated the gritty taste of the protein powder, he'd tried combinations of bananas, nuts, syrups, and juices to disguise it. Later, after he researched vitamins and minerals himself, his concoctions got even crazier—with raw greens, berries you never heard of, and even some kind of algae that comes from the deep dark reaches of a swamp.

I don't think Troy had recipes for these smoothies. He just threw ingredients in the blender with ice and hoped the results tasted good. On the days he made faces and choking noises, I figured they did not.

I am not a morning person, and the next day, as usual, I was running late. Jenny, Ralph, and Troy were in the kitchen when I charged in with my shoes untied and the buttons of my school jumper matched wrong. Jenny took one look, shook her head, came around the counter, and started putting me back together.

"You'll have to survive on a granola bar, Olivia," Jenny said. "There's a glass of milk right there for you. What've you done with your backpack?"

"I dunno. It must be somewhere, right? Upstairs?"

Jenny turned to face her husband, who was leaning

against the pantry door drinking coffee. "Ralph?" she said.

Ralph set the mug down on the counter and looked at me. "On your bed, do you think?" he asked.

"A very excellent place to start," I said.

Ralph left. Pouring the daily smoothie from the blender into a glass, Troy shook his head. "Sheesh, Livia, it's not rocket science to get ready for school. Most people don't have Ralph and Jenny to help out in the morning, you know."

"I do know," I said, "and I am very, very, very eternally super grateful every day of my life."

"Don't slather it on too thick," Jenny said. "You can eat the granola bar in the car. Are you about ready, Troy?" She looked over at him and started to laugh. "Oh my goodness," she said, so I looked over and saw his face and started laughing, too.

"*What?*" Troy scowled.

"What was in your smoothie this morning?" Jenny asked. "Raspberries or what?"

"Beets." Troy's eyes shot from Jenny to me. "*What?*"

"You're sporting a fine-looking hot pink 'stache, my friend," Jenny said, and before he could do a thing to get rid of it, I had whipped out my phone and snapped a picture.

Ralph came back at that moment, explaining he had found my backpack on my pink love seat, buried beneath a pile of shoes, coats, and hoodies. Meanwhile, Troy came at me, trying to grab my phone, and Jenny went at him with a damp cloth to wipe his face.

"Delete that right now!" my brother demanded.

"As soon as I post it," I said, dancing backward.

"Oh, whatever." Troy stopped so Jenny could clean him up. "Who cares what your friends think? We're gonna be late. Come on."

By lunchtime, the picture of Troy Baron rocking a pink mustache had fifteen shares and 128 likes.

When I checked after school, it had two hundred shares and more than twenty-five hundred likes.

By the time Mom called me for dinner, it had almost three thousand shares and more than thirty-five thousand likes.

I thought my phone was going to blow up!

Since the very first time I ever snapped a selfie, I had hoped for this kind of super-colossal response. Well, now I had it—and a gigantic expanding ocean of followers, too.

It was exciting. . . . It was a disaster.

Like he wasn't self-centered and stuck-up enough already, my brother had gone viral.

CHAPTER TWENTY-SIX

Olivia

The photo, I have to admit, was pretty funny.

It was a close-up of Troy's face, tilted, wild-eyed, protesting—his tongue out trying to taste his smoothie mustache, which stretched from one corner of his mouth to the other and reached almost to his nose. In real life, it had been brilliant magenta, but it was *startling* magenta after my rock-'em-sock-'em editing. In a thoughtless hurry, I had written a caption: *Troy Baron and his pink smoothie 'stache.*

Still in school that same day, I got suspicious that something was going on because girls I barely knew started mentioning how my brother is cute, and I had to think. *Why are they telling me this now?*

Then, later on, kids started asking about smoothies. Does my brother make them himself? Are they always pink?

Even before I saw the numbers, a sneaky plan started forming in my head. My brother had always been known for being smart, a good athlete, and good-looking, too. Well, what if he got even better known for something ridiculous?

Besides, Christmas was over, school was easy, and the spring session of After-School Acting Studio wouldn't start for another couple of weeks. As Jenny would say, I needed a project to keep me out of trouble.

I didn't see Troy till that evening when we all sat down to dinner. Jenny served our plates as usual. By this time, I'd forgotten all about baseball. The online frenzy had wiped it clean out of my head.

"Who would like to—," my mother began.

"I'll give thanks!" I said.

"Nice to see some enthusiasm," my father said.

"Isn't it?" I said. "And now, let us bow our heads in prayer. Heavenly father above, thank you for Jenny and Ralph, without whose help I would never make it to school in the morning. Thank you for my youthful, loving, and generous parents. Thank you for the food we eat, even if it is healthy. And thank you most of all for Troy Baron, my strong, handsome, smart, and viral brother. In Jesus's name we pray. Amen."

I looked up to see Troy and my parents all staring at me. "What?" I said. "And isn't it cheating to open your eyes before the 'amen'?"

"Did you just tell God I'm handsome?" my brother asked.

"Strong and smart, too," I said.

"And what was the other thing—viral?" my mom said. "You mean like viraling on social media?"

I rolled my eyes. "*Mo-o-om!* Nobody says viral-*ing*."

"Whatevs," said Mom. "Does this have something to do with that picture of Troy I saw on my screen today?

I didn't click, though. Who has that much time?"

I said, "Only everyone I ever met." Then I explained about the mustache post. "You saw it, right?" I said to Troy. "Your friends were all over sharing it."

Troy shrugged. "Were they? Some girls maybe. But you're up to something, Livia. You would never be so nice if you weren't."

I threw my hand to my forehead and collapsed back in my chair. "How *can* you be so cruel? I am your loving sister!"

"Save the Shakespeare for Acting Studio," my brother said. "Now, what's going on? How worried should I be?"

"Not a bit worried." I straightened up. "But it's true I have a *teeny*-tiny request. From now on, could you every morning drink your smoothie like usual, then let me take a picture of you, same as I did today. It would help if you made your smoothies colorful. Otherwise, the mustache won't show up. What do you say? Deal?"

This whole conversation had happened between bites of Jenny's very healthy pasta, which had spinach in it along with little round beans and salty cheese. Since Troy and I had done most of the talking, there was a lot on our plates, but my dad's was almost empty. I noticed now that he was looking intently at what was left—possibly searching for red meat.

My brother shook his head. "I don't think so, Livia. It would feel creepy to put my face out there for everyone to see and maybe laugh at. Besides, it's not like I've done anything good to deserve attention. I just look goofier than usual when I'm smeared with a pink mustache."

"Everyone deserves attention!" I said. "And here in the twenty-first century, if you want to claim your fair share, you can't just sit on your behind. You've got to take action."

"You mean take pictures," Troy said.

"Or videos," I said.

"How do you know all this, Livia?" my mother asked.

"Everyone does," I said, "unless they live in a cave—no offense."

My mother looked at my father. "Now that I think of

it," she said, "didn't we just hire a kid to handle social media for Baron Barbecue? Rae-Lyn in marketing thought it would be a good idea. I believe the girl we hired is named Jessica."

"And she's a kid?" I pictured a third grader behind a desk. She had red lipstick and a good manicure. Over her shoulder was an ostrich-skin messenger bag. On her feet were stilettos. This person did not actually exist. I had invented her from nothing. Still, I felt very, very jealous.

"Not a *kid* kid," my father clarified. "In fact, a young woman with an advanced degree."

"You can go to college for Facebook?" I said.

"More or less," my father said. "Maybe you would like a job like that someday."

"Livia could have that job now," Troy said.

"Totally!" I said.

"You do spend too much time on your phone, Livia," my father said.

"How come for me it's too much time and for Jessica it's a job?" I asked.

"Got you there, Dad," said Troy.

My father dabbed the corner of his mouth with his napkin. "As a matter of fact, she does not," he said, and the way he looked at my brother, I could tell the baseball fight lived on. "Jessica is doing social media on behalf of a company that employs hundreds of people and provides satisfaction to millions. Livia is doing it only for herself."

"Myself *and* my brother," I said, and added very sweetly, "*if* he'll let me. Besides, all my friends do it too."

I knew as soon as I said it that this last argument was bad, and—colossal surprise alert!—my father pounced. "If all your friends jumped off a cliff—," he began.

"Yes!" I cut him off. "Yes, I would jump too! Because life would not be worth living if none of my friends were left."

"Don't exaggerate, Olivia," said my mother.

"I'm not," I said.

"Enough," said my father. "Troy, I am with you a hundred percent on this one. Who would want to look at photos of my son with a dirty face?"

"Thousands of people!" I said. "And that was before dinner. *If* I were allowed to look at my phone, I could give you the updated figures."

"The whole thing is nonsense," said my father—and I bet he expected that to be the end of it, too—but it wasn't because Troy surprised us both.

"On the other hand, Livvy"—he looked at me—"it's really no skin off my nose if you want to take a photo of me every morning. I mean, I'm gonna be drinking my smoothie anyway."

"Seriously?" I was ecstatic beyond measure. I wanted to jump up, run around the table, and throw my arms around my one and only brother, except I knew that this would never fly with the politeness police—aka my parents. So all I did was tell him, "*Thank you, thank you, thank you, thank you—*"

My brother raised both hands. "Okay, okay, Livvy. You've made your point. And you'll have to come downstairs on time in the morning and remember your backpack, too, you know. I can't be late to school.

I have AP history first, and Mr. Nordquist's tardiness policy is zero-tolerance."

"I will. I swear," I said, and crossed my heart. "What kind of smoothie tomorrow, do you think?"

"Hmmm," said Troy. "I'm thinking mint."

CHAPTER TWENTY-SEVEN

Olivia

During the rest of dinner, my dad was glum and silent. It was the whole baseball thing and besides that—I'm guessing—he really, really, *really* wanted to make a new rule forbidding our posting smoothie mustaches every day. The trouble was he couldn't think of a good reason for the rule, and as strict as my dad is, he is rarely unreasonable.

For dessert we ate the last of Hannah's delicious

lemon cookies. You know the miracle of the loaves and fishes in the Bible that multiply to feed thousands? That must be exclusively a Jesus thing because in my own personal experience sharing makes things disappear faster.

I was looking longingly at the last crumbs and sugar sparkles on my plate when my mother asked whether I'd written to Hannah yet to thank her.

"Mom!" I protested. "The cookies only got here a couple of days ago, and you know how busy I am!"

My mother raised her eyebrows. "I didn't mean to criticize, Olivia. I only meant that if you haven't, please tell her how much we all enjoyed them."

"Oh," I said. "Sorry, Mom. Okay."

"Are you still thinking you'll go back to Moonlight Ranch this year?" Mom asked.

"Totally," I said.

"That's good to hear," said my dad, speaking up for the first time in a while. "I can't call your summer camp inexpensive, Livia, but apart from your own enjoyment, the cookies have made it a good investment."

Please do not think that I, Olivia Baron, am some ungrateful, ill-mannered wretch.

But the fact is almost a whole month passed before I got around to writing that thank-you note to Hannah, and I only did it then because I was looking for my homework folder and, as I delved deeply into the pile of papers, pens, lipsticks, snow globes, barrettes, markers, ink pads, origami paper, Legos, beauty products, stickers, books, PEZ dispensers, et cetera, et cetera, on top of my desk, I happened to uncover Hannah's letter.

Oh my gracious sakes, did I feel *terrible*!

What *must* my most favorite and benevolent counselor think of me?

Also, what Hannah, Jack, and Travis episode had I missed?

To assuage the torments of my conscience, I determined to write back posthaste!

Also, writing to Hannah would be a lot more pleasant than writing my report on the Gateway Arch, Symbol of Westward Expansion.

Since my bed was at that moment an unusable tangle

of sheets, covers, and pillows, I made myself a nest in my biggest, most comfortable chair and began.

Sunday, February 12

Dearest, most beautiful, most brilliant, wise and knowledgeable Hannah, far and away and beyond dispute the best counselor at Moonlight Ranch!

Je suis désolé (which means "I'm sorry" in case you took Spanish or Japanese or something) that I have not written till now to thank you for the utterly fantabulous and perfect in every way sparkly lemon cookies, which my entire family loved like crazy and devoured like the locusts in the Old Testament devoured the crops of the Egyptians.

I have been so, so, so very busy. Since you are a fan of smoothie 'stache I will not bother to explain in detail but will only say: It is hard work creating a social media sensation! My

brother and I (with help from Jenny) have to
plan all recipes, all ingredients, and all the poses
for the pictures. I have to (quelle horreur!) get
up early. I have to deal with constant requests
from friends who either want sneak previews
of recipes, or for me to take their own
pictures with mustaches made from chocolate
pudding, or marker, or school-cafeteria soup.

(I tell them no. I can't dilute the brand.)

The good part is all the likes. I even made
a red and pink graph of them and got extra
credit in math class.

The bad part is that some people are really
mean and post very personal comments, not
only about recipes but also about Troy's skin
color, his hair, and the shape of his nose. Troy
says, "Don't read them, Livvy. Don't dignify
racism and ignorance with your attention."

But sometimes I can't help it, Hannah. And
I get a queasy stomach when I do.

Change of topic, to quote the esteemed

Lucy's esteemed and beautiful mother—because
that one is too sad and depressing.

Not to be nosy, but what happened to Jack?
The Cookie Club membership were unanimous in
favor!

In other news from here in America's
heartland: Troy quit the baseball team a
month ago, and my poor dad is still upset, so
now there is basically an acrimonious debate
(aka a fight) at dinner every night about who
should run things, old people with experience or
young people with new ideas. My mother calls
this healthy discussion. I call it BORING and
AWKWARD.

As for my own romantic life, I was
interested in this math genius named Richard
but now find myself way, way, WAY too busy
for such trifles.

Mrs. W at After-School Acting Studio
has picked Little Red Riding Hood for the
spring play. We try out for parts in a couple

of weeks. I think I will look good in red, don't you? (LOL!)

Love ya lots and lots and lots and see you in a very, very, VERY few short months!

The one, the only, the incomparable: Olivia!!!

P.S. Do you know if Buck, in his infinite wisdom, is going to make that silly, silly rule about no phones at camp again this summer?

That was a good letter, I decided after I read it over. Jenny was right. It was amazing what a girl could do if she put her mind to it. I folded the stationery neatly in three and laid the letter on top of the pile on my desk. I could dig out Hannah's address and an envelope later. Right now there were metrics to check.

CHAPTER TWENTY-EIGHT

P.S.

Olivia

The creative team—Jenny, Troy, Ralph, and I—agreed the Valentine's Day smoothie should be as red as red could be, and it took several experiments before we got it right. The winning formula used three different berries as well as a soupçon (look it up!) of paprika, to fix the color. Also, according to my brother the mustache model, paprika is good for the pain-free well-being of knees, elbows, ankles, and shoulders, all of which take a beating if you happen to be an athlete.

I don't know if it was the quality of the red mustache or my brother's pose in a heart-shaped frame, but our metrics that day were the best yet. Apparently, my one and only brother, Troy Baron, now qualified as a bona fide heartthrob.

Can you say *gross?*

Can you say *it's your own fault, Olivia?*

And maybe that's the grossest part of all.

On the day after Valentine's Day—a day that will live in infamy, to borrow a phrase from some president or other—I first saw North Dakota Kitten. It was on Esmee Snyder's feed, of course.

Of course you saw it too. Everybody did. But in case you've forgotten, I'll remind you that the first one was fluffy and black, looking up from a dish of ice cream, its face half covered in the melted stuff.

Okay, it was cute—but also a total rip-off of smoothie 'stache. I mean, why didn't the content creator just call it kitten 'stache and be done with it? To add insult to injury, the post included a recipe (Hello? A *recipe?!*) for the ice cream, which was fish flavor, made for felines.

I think I commented "Cute!" and reposted just to keep Esmee on my good side. We were going to be competing for the part of Little Red at Acting Studio, and I didn't want her to be too mad when she lost out.

The smoothie 'stache numbers fell a little after that, but I wasn't worried—not yet—and on St. Patrick's Day, they bounced back. Troy had refused to go all head-to-toe leprechaun, but he did put on a cheesy cardboard hat with a gold foil buckle and green sequins.

"Hat's too small, Olivia," Ralph said that morning in the kitchen, looking him over. "Troy, you look silly."

Troy said, "Of *course* I look silly." He was staring into the blender and making a happy-astonished face, as if he had just found a pot of gold inside.

"Be quiet and hold still." I snapped a couple of extras for insurance. "There. You're good. Okay, Ralph. We can go to school. How did that one taste, Troy?"

Troy shrugged. "The wheatgrass is a little bland, but better than your idea, Livia. I'm pretty sure humans can't digest shamrocks."

Ironically (upside-down coincidence, remember?), I seemed to have less time to participate in social media now that I was creating social media. Like normally after school, I used to chat here, snap there, watch this video and play that game, but now I always seemed to have work to do. The next day, for example, I was reading up on mulberries for the April Fool's smoothie when I got a text from Emma. Of the four of us—Grace, Lucy, Emma, and me—she's the nicest *and* the bossiest. Could a career as preschool teacher be in her future? Magic 8 Ball says: Yes.

Emma: Hey, beautiful and talented friend O— how doin'? Are you ready for some 😊 ?

Olivia: Yes yes yes yes yes yes YES! ✏️

Emma: How RU?

Olivia: Busy busy busy. 🐝

Emma: I bet! BTW, your brother is handsome. ♡♡ All my friends in ♡. I ♡ how his left ear is a tiny bit pointed.

Olivia: That's gross, Emma, and it's because he's half 😈

Emma: Uh-oh. Are you not getting along again?

Olivia: Again—wha'?????

Emma: Like last year, remember? I told you about Nathan?

Olivia: Right! The cookies were chocolate. Big bro and I OK. It's my dad who is a big 😀 —all Mr. Pouty Pants since Troy quit baseball.

Emma: Poor Dad.

Olivia: No!!! Poor Troy. And poor, poor, POOR Olivia!!!! Anyway, now Easter's coming and we have to go to Pop-Pop and Mama's, and Dad-Troy will probably fight.

Emma: Cookies to stop a fight?

Olivia: An Easter 🏁 fight.

Emma: Hey gtta go! Shopping w/ Grandma. ☹

Olivia: ????? Who doesn't like to shop?

Emma: Me! Love ya, O!

Olivia: Love ya, too!

After that I rechecked our metrics, answered a text, deleted some spam, decided against mulberries, and looked at the day's post from North Dakota Kitten. The kitten was spotted and the recipe was catnip sorbet—like that was so original. All the time something about Emma and Easter was bugging me.

Then I remembered—oy vey!—and slapped my forehead and dropped back into the chair.

Emma is Jewish!

And Jews don't even celebrate Easter.

What did she know about Easter cookies? Had I hurt her feelings by bringing it up?

CHAPTER TWENTY-NINE

Olivia

Was it really North Dakota Kitten?

Or did the world have a finite appetite for photos of my brother with a smeared-on mustache?

Either way, the metrics fell off a cliff at the beginning of April. Hoping for a bump, my creative team—Troy, Jenny, and Ralph—tried everything from yoga poses to fright wigs. We even sweetened up the smoothie recipes with caramel syrup and ice cream.

Still the numbers dropped.

Meanwhile, auditions for *Little Red Riding Hood* were the second week of April. The year before when we did *The Princess and the Pea*, yours truly starred as Princess Winifred while Esmee Snyder played the evil queen. (I would never stoop to claiming either was typecasting, but there were those who did—just sayin'.)

This year at tryouts, I walked offstage and handed over the red cape totally confident that my reading had nailed the full emotional range of the plucky but vulnerable hero who puts Grandma's needs first and—prepared to make the ultimate sacrifice—ventures into the woods, a picnic basket on her arm.

The next day Mrs. W posted the cast list—and I didn't get the part.

Esmee Snyder did.

So now you're thinking surely Olivia was cast as Grandma, then? Or hey, how about the wolf? That would be creative casting. You go, Mrs. W!

But I didn't get those parts either.

Instead, I, Olivia Baron, was cast as Second Chipmunk.

And if you're racking your brain trying to remember

Second Chipmunk from the fairy tale, you will fail because there are no chipmunks in the fairy tale. Like the sparrows, mice, and foxes, the chipmunks were added to the script by Mrs. W to ensure that everyone who pays tuition to After-School Acting Studio gets a part, even people so stage-frightened they can barely open their mouths to speak.

The cast list went up on Thursday afternoon. By Friday I had kind of expected one of my parents would phone Mrs. W to explain to her the magnitude of her mistake. That, I happen to know, is what Esmee Snyder's mother did the time Esmee was cast as the beanstalk.

But my mother said that playing a chipmunk, especially *second* chipmunk, would be a nice lesson in humility for someone who sometimes seemed to need one. (Could she possibly have meant me?) And my father laughed and said, "This I gotta see."

The next day, Saturday, I woke up mad with very little to do.

Smoothie 'stache was a weekday thing. We didn't go to baseball games anymore. Red Riding Hood rehearsal wasn't till two—the one for those of us cast as minor characters, that is. The kids playing leads had to be there at noon.

I yanked my sheets and stomped around my room and checked the metrics again and chatted with Courtney, who also goes to Acting Studio. She had been cast as Little Red's mother, which was less minor than a chipmunk for heaven's sake but still pretty minor. And Courtney wasn't even mad about it, either.

What is wrong with people anyway?

Around eleven, I arranged an old sweatshirt over my pajamas like a cape, grabbed my phone, and waltzed and pirouetted down the stairs, across the hall, through the dining room, and into the kitchen.

I was a little dizzy by the time I got there.

"Good morning, sleepyhead," said Jenny.

"Good morning, Jenny," I said. "Not that it *is* a good morning. Tell me, please, do you know the whereabouts of my dear, dear parents?"

"Your dad had to go in to the office for a few hours," Jenny said, "and your mom has a meeting. What would you like for breakfast?"

"A few sunflower seeds, I guess. Maybe a worm or two. I believe that's appropriate food for chipmunks, is it not?" I asked.

Jenny laughed. "I hate to think what you'd ask for if you were playing the wolf. How about oatmeal? It's chilly for April, and oatmeal will warm you up."

"Don't go to any trouble, Jenny," I said. "I am only a minor character, after all."

Troy must've slept late, too, because now he came in behind me and laughed. "Give it a rest, Olivia," he said. "I would love some oatmeal, Jenny. Hold the worms."

Jenny makes oatmeal on the stove, not in the microwave, and she puts real cream on top, too. This is another of those things my friends can't believe when they stay over.

After breakfast I felt better. I would read for a while. I would scheme improvements for smoothie 'stache. I would watch TV. I would watch a dozen new cat videos—but not North Dakota Kitten, anything but North Dakota Kitten.

With these gritty, positive, can-do thoughts in my head, I told Jenny thank you for the lovely, lovely oatmeal, rearranged my sweatshirt cape, and prepared to pirouette back upstairs.

Then Troy said, "Livvy? I need to talk to you."

CHAPTER THIRTY

Olivia

The motto on the salt box says, when it rains, it pours.

OMG—don't I know it.

In the course of two short days, I not only became a minor character, but I became a minor character without a significant social media platform.

"Dad's right," I told Troy when he announced he didn't want to do smoothie 'stache anymore. "You *are* a quitter!"

"I'm not," he said, so calm and reasonable he about made me want to jump out of my chair. "It's just that it's run its course is all," he went on. "Even a good-looking face like mine can't draw traffic forever. Besides, I'm bored posing for pictures every morning, and I don't like pushing sugar either."

We were in my brother's room, a place I am rarely permitted to enter even though it's only three doors down from my own with the furniture arranged the same way, too—sitting area, bookcases, and a desk on one side, queen-size bed on the other. On my brother's walls are baseball plaques and photos. On his shelves are trophies. The posters are mostly sports teams—the Royals, the Chiefs, the Jayhawks, and the Tigers.

"Well, just imagine how I feel," I said. "My whole point was to make you look ridiculous and instead I made you into a star."

"That was your whole point?" my brother said.

"That and getting likes," I said.

"I don't get that either," my brother said. "Why do you care about likes?"

I took a breath and blew it out. Troy had to be the most exasperating brother since Cain. Also, clueless. "How do I even answer a question like that? Why not ask me why I breathe, or why I shop, or why I like that cute boy Richard in math class who officially does not care about me at all?"

"You breathe to stay alive, Olivia," Troy said.

"Same reason I collect likes," I said, "to stay alive *socially.* If someone gets more likes than me, I'm socially in the toilet."

Troy made a face. *"Ew,"* he said. "I guess it's a girl thing. But as for making me look ridiculous—why bother? Most of the time I have no trouble doing that for myself."

"Are you kidding?" I said. "Around here you have always been Mr. Perfect, and then you went and quit baseball and you weren't Mr. Perfect anymore, but you were still one hundred percent the center of attention. All anyone wanted to talk about was how you quit baseball. It's all you and Dad still talk about. I'm sick of it. Who cares about—"

"Livvy?" my brother interrupted. "Give it a rest, okay?

I know it's not fair. Baseball was way too big a deal around here. And there's something else, too, but you have to promise you'll never tell Dad and Mom."

I was revved up and ready to argue, but now Troy was acting so serious that I took a breath and slowed down. "I give my solemn oath," I said, and drew an X across my chest.

"Okay." Troy took a breath too. "Here's the thing. Coach wasn't all that broken up when I told him I was quitting."

I let that sink in for a moment but still didn't understand. Everybody knew my brother was a baseball star. Of course his quitting would hurt the team. "What do you mean?" I asked.

"I used to be a pretty good player, it's true. I knew the game inside and out because I'd been playing my whole life, but my real advantage was size. I grew up earlier than the other guys, so I was stronger than them and faster, too.

"Well, guess what, Livvy? The other guys caught me, and now I'm more like average. There's a sophomore this year who played JV last year—Malik. Coach just loves him. With me out of the way, Malik is starting, and doing better than I would've."

"Why not tell Dad this?" I asked. "What's the big secret?"

Troy shrugged. "Maybe it's just my stupid ego. I want Dad to think I'm still a star—going out on a high note. Anyway, Dad would just tell me I'm lazy. I should try harder."

"He's right," I said.

Troy shook his head. "He wasn't out there. I was, and I know. Anyway, where was baseball going to take me? The last superstar from my high school was a pitcher. He played a year in the minors for peanuts, then messed up his shoulder real bad. Now all that's left is a dusty plaque on the wall of the high school locker room—big deal.

"I miss the guys and I miss the excitement, Livvy, but I had to be realistic," Troy concluded. "Don't laugh, but I'm better off spending time on my homework. I wish Dad would get that."

"Smoothie 'stache doesn't interfere with your home-work," I said. "And I have a lot of great ideas to regain eyeballs, like making it more interactive. So from now on, every day you walk in mud or glue or something. And then we post your footprints, and people have to guess what you stepped in. What do you think?"

Troy frowned. "I think I'm stuck to the floor going nowhere," he said. "Nope, I'm done. You know in the Bible where Paul tells the Corinthians to put away childish things? That is what I am doing."

If Troy had been all angry and loud, I would have fought back. But he wasn't, and his cool made me think he would never change his mind.

So I gave up and stood up. "Try the Bible out on Dad," I suggested.

"Maybe I will," he said.

CHAPTER THIRTY-ONE

Olivia

And now let us turn from childish things to cheerful ones—like how my dear, dear, wonderful friend Emma was so totally punctual with the Easter cookies, which arrived on Good Friday. Later, when I looked at the calendar, I saw why. It was one of those years when Passover and Easter overlapped.

Since I go to Catholic school, we had Good Friday off. I think Jenny was almost as excited as me when the UPS guy rang the bell after lunch and we saw the return address on the box: Gladwyne, PA.

"They were chocolate last year, weren't they?" Jenny said as she carried the package into the kitchen. I was right behind her.

"With icing," I said. "If I close my eyes, I can still taste them."

Jenny set the package down and handed me a knife. "Be careful, Olivia," she said.

I gave her the knife back. "You will do a much better job."

Three swift cuts later, the box was open and the cookies had been set free—macaroons! And not just any macaroons either, but chocolate-dipped macaroons with chocolate squiggles on top.

"You don't happen to be one of those coconut haters, do you, Jenny?" I asked.

"You know I love coconut," she said. "Why?"

"Too bad." I sighed a grand dramatic sigh. "I was hoping more for me."

"Very funny," Jenny said. "But we should save them for later—shouldn't we?"

"We should save most of them," I said.

Mustering superhuman willpower and self-control, Jenny and I restricted our cookie consumption to two each. After that, the plan was for Ralph to drive me to Courtney's to hang out till dinner, but first I wanted to change my clothes. I was on my way upstairs when Jenny called, "Hang on, sweetheart. I didn't notice till now, but there's a letter."

11 April, Tuesday

Dear dear dearest, most brilliant, brainy, and talented O!

I am sending macaroons for your Easter party because they are traditional cookies for Passover. (Maybe you knew that?) Same as matzo and other Passover foods, they don't have flour and leavening, which aren't allowed this time of year. Why aren't they allowed?

I will tell you.

The idea is we remember the Jews who didn't have time to hang out waiting for their bread (or cookies!) to rise when they were escaping from Pharaoh three thousand years ago.

How are you? Are you surviving baseball? Is smoothie 'stache on break? My friends and I all miss it. ☹☹☹ You have to bring it back!

I am fine and school is good, but things have not been that great around my house this year because my great-grandmother died in January :☹:, and after that my mom got depressed and wouldn't get out of bed, which was just so weird. She is a little better now—back at work and she goes to a counselor. She says she wants to get well for her family because she loves us, but sometimes she still feels sad.

I thought I understood grown-ups, but it turns out I don't.

Another strange thing has happened around my house, but this one isn't necessarily terrible. Are you ready? We all believe in ghosts!

It started when Grace sent cookies to help my mom, and I made some more, and I think indirectly the cookies did help my mom (she got out of bed), but then the strange thing happened: A ghost came and ate most of them.

Go ahead and think I'm crazy if you want.

It's possible it was our dog or that someone took the cookies as a joke, but I prefer the idea that my brother Nathan's ghost was with us for a few minutes, gobbling cookies the way a kid might. My mom says she likes the idea too.

So score one for flour power? I

haven't written Hannah yet to tell her
this weird story.

Speaking of Hannah—did she send you
cookies? Did she tell you about how Jack
broke up with her?

I am not sure I agree with you that
romance is so great, O. It seems to
cause one crisis after another. If we
have to sneak into Boys Camp again this
summer, you guys are on your own. My
parents will make me come home for sure
if I break my ankle again!

Sorry if this letter is too weird or too
serious or too long. I am just telling you
the truth about what's going on—it has
been a very strange year so far.

Love always from one of your Moonlight
Ranch besties, Emma

P.S. Here is something ironic! These

cookies are supposed to deliver flour power
for your Easter celebration, but the
truth is they have no flour!

P.P.S. Your turn to write to Lucy. And
remember: She has no phone, so she has
never even heard of smoothie 'stache!

I read Emma's letter once and thought she was
crazy, then a second time and thought I was mean
for thinking she was crazy. Her poor mom! And poor
Emma, too! In my life lately, the very worst things were
one pouty-pants dad and one social-media calamity.
In Emma's life, someone she loved had died, her mom
was sad, and her brother's ghost had come back to
haunt them.

Except that couldn't be right, could it? Nobody
believes in ghosts.

My phone buzzed. My tablet flashed. I ignored them
and thought of Emma—of how she must be feeling . . .
but a person can only ignore their phone for so long,

right? Courtney was texting. She probably thought I'd forgotten all about her.

OMW, I typed back.

"O-LIV-*ee*-yah?" Jenny called up the stairs.

"Be right there!" I called. Then I dropped Emma's letter and opened a dresser drawer. What had I done with my new jeans anyway?

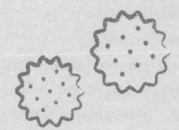

CHAPTER THIRTY-TWO

Olivia

Mama and Pop-Pop are my father's parents. They live near the river, only a few miles from our house, but the neighborhood—same one where my dad grew up—is totally different and not as nice. The houses are small. There aren't many trees. Some of the yards are over-grown with weeds.

My parents have offered to buy my grandparents a place closer to our house, a big condo in a nice building—elevator, doorman, the works!—but my grandparents won't budge.

After church on Sunday morning—Easter—Mom, Dad, Troy, and I drove over to have brunch. I was wearing my church clothes, a pink lace dress with a full skirt and pink wedge sandals. I looked good, if I do say so myself. My mom and I had certainly shopped long enough. Anyway, the only trouble was that the sash had a bow and on the car ride that dug into my back. When I got home I would probably find a bruise as big as Alaska.

I wanted to ask why, oh why, we had to drive all the long, long way over to my grandparents' house instead of inviting them to ours—except I knew the answer would be a steely look from my dad and a *hush now* from my mother.

So I tried a different approach.

"Why is it they don't want to move again?" I asked.

"Pop-Pop says we should save our money instead of wasting it on something fancy for a couple of old people," said Troy, who was fiddling with the remote for the sound system in the SUV. "He says you never know when a rainy day will come and you might need it."

"Good advice," said my father, glancing back at us in the rearview mirror.

My mother looked over her shoulder. "That's what he and Mama *say,* but I think the truth is that they're stubborn and don't like change—just like their son."

"Me? Stubborn?" Dad said.

"They don't even hardly visit us," I said. "If they lived closer, we could see them more."

"They feel funny in our neighborhood," Troy said. "When it was first built, black people weren't even allowed to live there."

"That can't be true," I said. "Where did you hear that?"

"It is true," Dad said. "When your grandparents were young, there were restrictions that said only white people could buy property there. Those restrictions had been illegal for years by the time your mom and I bought, but attitudes don't always change with the laws."

I know about slavery and the Civil Rights movement

and discrimination and Black Lives Matter. I know racism is a real thing, in other words—and if I needed a reminder, I got it from the comments on smoothie 'stache. But all of that, even the comments, seemed far away compared with discrimination against my very own grandparents. I got a queasy feeling in my stomach, and all I could do was swallow and hope it went away.

"Here we are now," Dad said. "Don't forget your manners, you two, or I'll never hear the end of it."

Dad turned into the driveway and, as if they'd been watching at the window, my grandparents appeared on the front porch, smiling and waving. I rolled down my window, waved back, and hollered, "Hello!"

Whether it's Christmas or your birthday or Fourth of July, Mama makes macaroni and cheese, biscuits, coleslaw, green beans, fruit salad, deviled eggs, and a sheet cake. So that's what she made for Easter brunch, too, and Jenny had sent along ribs. We ate till we had to stop, and then Pop-Pop brought Troy and me Easter baskets full of chocolate eggs and jelly beans.

"No more!" Troy laughed. "I'll burst and you'll have to clean up the mess."

"Troy?" my mother said.

"Sorry, Mom," Troy said, "and you're right. Livia should clean up. Mama and Pop-Pop have done more than their share."

"You're not funny," I said.

"He is kind of funny," Pop-Pop said. "But I was sorry to hear you quit the baseball team, Troy."

My mother rose from her chair abruptly and grabbed the nearest plates. "I'll clear up," she said. "You all just sit and visit."

My father frowned at my brother. "We were all sorry," he said. Would he ever get over it?

Troy kept his voice even. "I know a lot of people were disappointed, but it had to be done. It was time."

Mom came back for more plates. It was strange to see her doing Jenny's job. "Awfully quiet in here," she said. "Is everything okay?"

Dad said "Fine" without looking up.

I said, "Do you want help, Mom?" Partly I was being

my usual kind and generous self. Partly I wanted to avoid another round of Dad versus Troy.

"No, no," Mom said. "I'll let you know if I need you," and then she returned to the kitchen.

The silence that followed was awkward, but it didn't last. Soon Mom was back. "Olivia, can you believe we forgot these?" She was carrying a plate of macaroons.

"Where did these come from?" Mama wanted to know, and I explained.

"Can't turn that down, then," Mama said, reaching for one, and it turned out nobody else could either, full as we were.

Pop-Pop had just swallowed the last morsel of his when he started to chuckle. "You know, Troy," he said, "the way you spoke just now—it reminded of a certain young man who used to live in this very house."

"Oh, now"—Dad shook his head, but he looked less stern than he had before—"don't you go telling tales on me, Pop."

"B'lieve I might. It's the prerogative of age. Don't you agree, Olivia?"

"Sure," I said. "I like your stories about my dad. Is it the one about the broken window? That's my favorite, but I like the one about all the strawberries, too."

"This one will be new to you, I think," said Pop-Pop.

"Oh my," said my father.

Pop-Pop looked at Mama for permission. She shrugged one shoulder—just the way Troy does.

"This is the story," Pop-Pop began, "of the time your father quit something, himself."

CHAPTER THIRTY-THREE

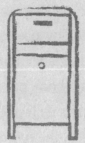

Olivia

Pop-Pop's story: "You kids may not know this, but your dad's first job title was not so exalted as the one he has today. It was paper boy. This was back in the day, you understand, when everybody subscribed to the morning paper, and they expected it on their doorstep even before they perked their coffee.

"Your dad was only ten years old when he got his first route, and he was up before the sun rose to walk that route and deliver those papers in every kind of bad Kansas City weather.

"It was hard work for low pay, especially at first, when he was younger and smaller than most of the other boys. The newspapers didn't pay you by the hour—oh no—they paid by papers delivered. So how it went was the more you delivered, the more you earned, and the faster you delivered, the faster you earned.

"Well, as all boys do, your father grew, and as *some* boys do, your father worked hard. By the time he was fourteen years old, I'd wager to say he was the fastest and best-paid paper boy in all of Kansas City. He knew the newspaper delivery business cold.

"But then came the summer he turned sixteen, an especially hot summer if I remember correctly. Your dad was going into his junior year in high school, and he announced that he was quitting his paper route.

"'I want to do something new,' he told your mama and me.

"Well, now, being the wise, practical, and conservative father that I am, I discouraged him in no uncertain terms. 'You got a sure thing going, son,' I told him, 'something you're good at. You got your pocket money and some savings besides. Why would you want to mess with that? Not to mention, what is it you're going to do with yourself?'

"'I'm not sure,' your dad answered. 'I just know I want to do something different.'

"This, I came to believe later on, was a crock o' malarkey. He knew exactly what he wanted to do. He just did not want to let on at that time.

"Now, being as how you know what happened later, it might be you think you know where this is going. No one can deny that George Baron has done real well with his barbecue sauce. Maybe you're anticipating he wanted to spend some time in the kitchen.

"But that wasn't it. That came later. What had captured his fancy was baseball. Our own Kansas City Royals had won the World Series that year, and the whole town was crazy for them. Your dad had never played more than pickup games in the park and stickball in the street, but he had a certain amount of natural athletic ability, and as I've already said, he was fast. He wanted to see if maybe he was good enough to play on a real team.

"If this was a movie, your dad would not only make the team, he'd be the best player on it and hit the winning home run in the championship game. In real life, he made the team, but only just, and he never played much. Most of the other boys were just plain better. In the end, they had too much of a head start on him when it came to skills and knowledge both.

"As for your mama and me, we came around after a while and even went to some of his games. It was fun for us and for him, too. If he regretted his choice—or the depletion of his savings—he never told us.

"The worst part was the new paper boy wasn't nearly as good as your daddy, and I missed my morning paper more times than I like to think about."

Done with his story, Pop-Pop reached for another cookie and chewed it thoughtfully.

Dad said, "I forgot we argued when I quit the paper route."

Pop-Pop said, "We did, and I didn't forget."

Then Troy turned to Dad. "You never told me you played ball."

Dad shrugged. "There wasn't much to say about warming the bench."

"So is that why you wanted me to play?" Troy asked. "Was I supposed to live your dream?"

"Now, Troy . . . ," Mom said. "It's a holiday. We are not going to fuss."

"I'm not fussing. I'm wondering." Troy was still looking at Dad.

Dad sighed. "I introduced you to baseball because I liked it as a kid, and I still do. Then you turned out to be good at it. Now you've quit. That's the end of that particular story, I guess. Maybe someday, far in the future, we will tell it around the table on Easter Sunday."

CHAPTER THIRTY-FOUR

Wednesday, May 10

Hannah retrieved the letter from her mailbox at the P.O., glanced at the return address, and smiled. It was a much-belated thank-you from Olivia—had to be.

When was it Hannah had sent those cookies to Olivia? January?

She hadn't heard a word, and now it was May, finals week, and here at last was a note back.

Hannah had a ton of studying to do. Why did those

Renaissance artists have to paint so much anyway? Couldn't they have contented themselves with a canvas or two each? No mere human could memorize it all, but she was headed to the library to try.

On the way, though, she bought an iced coffee at the student center, sat down at a patio table, and opened Olivia's note.

Monday, May 8

Dear kindest, most intelligent, brave, and princesslike secret-cookie friend Lucy,

Here is the news from chez moi.

You know (because I've told you) how my parents love my brother so much more than they love me????

Well, my brother quit baseball this year (!!!!), and since then he and I have actually been getting along. This is my theory: Without so much adulation and applause directed his way all the time, he has had the opportunity (at last!) to mature.

Praise the Lord!!!!

Ironically, however, just as he and I started to get along, he and my dad hit what Jenny calls a "rough patch," my mother calls "obstacles," and I call "glaring and arguing and making dinnertime SUPER unpleasant for everyone forced to sit through it."

But then (ta-da!) something happened.

Can you guess what?

FLOUR POWER!!!!

Emma sent macaroons for Easter, and while we ate them my pop-pop told a story about when my dad was a kid. At first it looked like this was only going to make Dad and Troy start up all over again, but then the flour power kicked in and Pop-Pop said, "Excuse me? If I may? You are both missing the point of my story. It wasn't about baseball at all. It was about quitting."

And my dad and Troy both said, "It was?" at practically the same instant.

And Pop-Pop said, "It was about how kids have to do what they have to do and how parents—even good ones such as myself and your dad—sometimes have to get outta the way and let them."

And my brother said, "Score!" and my dad said, "Hmph," and my mom and my grandmother both started to laugh, and then I did too—I think because we all realized how alike my dad and Troy really are. And last week when we went on family vacation, Dad and Troy skied together every day.

One more big news item before my typing fingers fall off and I have to call 911 using my toes. Did you get lemon cookies from Hannah yet? I'm sure you must have because she sent them to me and Grace and Emma. (I hope I remembered to send a thank-you note.) Anyway, did she tell you she's seeing Travis again?

I couldn't believe it either!!!!

After all the hard travail we went through

to piece that breakup letter together and
sneak cookies to Lance in Boys Camp and fix
her up with Jack, who is kind and nice besides
funny—how could she get back together with
that terrible, dreadful, no good, very bad
Travis? (LOL—I crack myself up.)

So now, Lucy my sweet cookie friend, write
and tell me ABSOLUTELY EVERYTHING
going on in your life! How are the triplets?
How is soccer? Have you strangled any wolves
with your bare hands lately? Are your mom and
your grandma okay? What about Vivek? Have
you heard from him? I promise I won't tell
Grace—my LIPS ARE SEALED!!!!

And most important of all, what do you
need FLOUR POWER to do for you?

Love always from your most favorite, most
funny, and most wise secret-cookie friend—O

CHAPTER THIRTY-FIVE

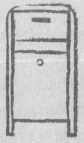

Wednesday, May 10, Lucy

Hello, O: It's Lucy, not spam! Please read this!

Something strange has happened. I got a letter from
you addressed to me, but it's really a thank-you note
to Hannah for cookies. It's dated February. (???) I
am forwarding to Hannah, no problem, but does this
mean you sent a letter for me to her?

No offense, but that sounds like something I would do.

I hope things are good.

And if you're wondering, I am borrowing Kendall's computer (she's Arlo, Mia, Levi, and Piper's mom), so that's how I'm e-mailing to you, but the one we had at home is still broken, and I still don't have a phone. If you can answer quick that's great because I'll be sitting at Kendall's desk for a few more minutes.

Love ya

—Lucy

I hit send and looked over my shoulder at Kendall, who was on the love seat nursing the baby, Piper. We were in her den. The triplets were in the family room watching *SpongeBob*—their absolute favorite—on TV.

"Thanks again," I said. "Maybe it wasn't a real emergency,

but I thought she ought to know what happened."

"You're welcome," Kendall said. "I'm glad you have such good friends from your camp, but we sure miss you in the summer. I guess you're going back for sure?"

"Aunt Freda says she can pay this year," I said. "It's good, 'cause I can save the money you've paid me for babysitting."

Kendall raised her eyebrows. "Wait a sec, Lucy. Do you mean last year you paid for camp with your babysitting money?"

"Mom helped some. It's no big deal," I said.

"Okay, but I'm impressed," Kendall said. "I never heard of a kid paying her own way to summer camp before."

I shrugged, wishing I hadn't said anything. My life is totally different from everybody else's in Beverly Hills— from everybody else's anywhere, maybe. My mom and I live with my nana, and my mom doesn't always work, and there's never money for anything extra. Usually, I don't bring it up.

"Oh, look." Kendall pointed her chin at the screen. "I think she answered."

OMG, hi, Lucy—Tx for letting me know. I hope I didn't say anything bad about Hannah in it. (Hahaha!) I wrote the letter by hand so no copy. In case she doesn't send it on—here is the important question. What do you need flour power to do for you? Xoxooxo!!!! O

"Do you mind if I write back one more time?" I asked Kendall.

"Of course I don't mind. The triplets are fine for a few more minutes. Then you can all go outside and chase each other till they drop from exhaustion. Are you sure you can't stay for dinner?" Kendall asked. "We would love to have you."

"I wish I could," I said sincerely, "but my mom's working, and Nana wants me home."

"Someday I'd like to meet your nana," Kendall said. "It's strange that I haven't when you only live down the block."

I said, "Oh, unh-hunh. Great idea." Then I turned back to the keyboard, thinking no way that meeting would ever happen. Nana—my grandmother—reads old books all day in a chair in her room and rarely goes outside. The reason she wanted me home was so I could make her dinner.

Hey, O—Glad you got that. I don't know what flour power can do about this, but there is news in my life too. My dad is back in town, and who knows what will happen? xoxox Gotta go wrangle triplets. See ya this summer!

So my life is different from other people's, and so is my family history.

My dad is almost twenty years older than my mom. Back when he had an important job and a lot of money, she quit college to marry him. She says she expected happily ever after, but that isn't how it went. When I was a baby, he did something wrong, something called *fraud*, and he had to go to prison. After that the money was gone, so Mom and I moved in with her mother, my nana.

It was awkward, my mom says. Nana never liked my father in the first place. Her own husband—my grandfather—had left her a long time before that, and she has been pretty much anti-men ever since.

By the time my father got out of prison, I was in kindergarten, and my mother didn't want to be married. I'm eleven now, and I haven't seen him since I was five, but sometimes he sends me cards, and sometimes the cards have cash in them. Once it was a ten-dollar bill. Written on the card is usually a cheerful "You go, girl!" kind of note that could have been for anyone.

My grandmother likes to remind me that it could be worse. I have a roof over my head (even if the bathroom ceiling leaks). I have enough to eat (provided I cook it myself). I have okay clothes (my mom is a good thrift-store shopper). I go to school like any other kid, and I even get to play soccer (because my coach makes sure I've got cleats and shin guards). For the last two years I've gotten to go to a fancy summer camp, too.

I have nothing to complain about, Nana says, and sometimes when I can't fall asleep and I'm sad, I repeat that over and over.

CHAPTER THIRTY-SIX

Lucy

I am good at two things, art and soccer. Coach Kamae says even though I entirely lack killer instinct, I have a knack for reading the field and kicking the ball where it needs to go. Playing soccer, I don't *think*; I just *do*—same with art. For me, things that require thinking are harder.

The afternoon after I e-mailed Olivia—Thursday— we had a game against the Eagles, the best team in our league, the team that goes to the playoffs every year.

Our team, the Bears, were "middling good," according to Coach Kamae, who always says what matters is to be "a nice group of young women working together in the fresh air and sunshine."

The serious parents are driven crazy by this attitude. They pull their girls to play for other teams, which doesn't help our roster any either. But whatever.

We lost 4–1 that day, and I scored our team's only goal—aiming my kick low on the ball so it would arc high and drop fast into the net behind the goalie, who spun around, confused, trying to figure out what had happened.

I had slipped around an Eagle fullback to take the shot. When it went in, the fullback looked disgusted. "Lucky!" she said, but it wasn't. I had kicked the ball just the way I meant to.

Usually Coach gives me a ride home, but that day I had actual fans in attendance. My mom was there, and so were Kendall and her kids. Somehow or another my mom had managed to stand on the wrong side, the visitor side. Kendall was with the rest of the Bears fans on the home side, so—after the "good game, good game, good game" ritual—I ran off the field toward her.

Piper the baby was in a sling across her chest. Arlo, Mia, and Levi came running toward me in a mass, grabbed my knees, and stayed put.

"Hi, hi, hi—thanks for coming!" I said.

"You were wonderful!" Kendall said.

"Oh. I guess. Was I? Thanks. But it looks like we lost anyway."

"You had a great game, though," Kendall said.

"Good game!" said Arlo.

"Dood dame!" said Levi.

"Good Lucy!" said Mia.

"Thanks, you guys." I dropped down to their level for a group hug. They smelled like jelly beans, grass, and salt.

"Mommy said next comes ice c'eam. C'mon, we go!" Arlo grabbed my right arm and almost pulled me over.

"Ice c'eam! Ice c'eam! Ice c'eam!" Levi and Mia chanted.

Kendall took a breath and squinched her eyes. "Sometimes I can't hear myself think."

"Think louder," I suggested just as my mom walked up.

"Did you see him?" Mom asked.

"Hi, Mom," I said. "I would like some ice cream, would you?"

"Your father, I mean," Mom said.

"Oh!" Kendall widened her eyes and looked at me.

"What? See who? I kicked a goal," I said.

"I'm sorry," my mom said. "I'm a little flustered. It's been so many years."

"No, it hasn't." I shook my head. "I kicked a goal at the game against the Fruit Bats, too. That was Monday—so only two days."

"I don't think that's what she means, Lucy," Kendall said. "I think she means your *father*."

"Have we met?" My mom turned to Kendall as if she had just noticed her, which was hard to believe. Kendall travels with four kids and all their stuff. She is hard to miss.

"Hi, KK." Kendall smiled. "I'm Kendall. We've met

before. We're neighbors, and your Lucy watches the kids for me after school. Wasn't that an exciting game? How about that daughter of yours?"

"Oh, of course," my mom said. "You'll have to excuse me. I'm kind of on the flustered side just now. My ex-husband had to leave abruptly and—"

"My dad?" I said. "He was *here*?"

Mom blinked. "Didn't I just say that?"

"Where did he go?" I asked, thinking back on the game. I had noticed my mother on the sidelines, but I didn't remember anyone with her. If it had been a man, I might not have paid attention, though. My mom goes through boyfriends like soccer players through Gatorade.

"He had a meeting. He says he's moving back to LA. Something big, he says—*huge*. If it all pans out, there're gonna be changes. That's what he says."

"Did he see me kick the goal?" I asked.

Mom shrugged. "Sure. Maybe."

"What kind of changes?" Kendall spoke to my mom, but she was looking at me.

"*Money* changes," my mom said in a hushed voice, like money was either secret or sacred.

Kendall breathed. "Oh, good. Because if you mean Lucy might move away—"

"*No-o-o-o!*" Levi wailed, which was the cue for Arlo and Mia to wail too. Then Piper in the sling joined the chorus.

"Now I've done it." Kendall bounced and patted Piper to soothe her. "Did somebody mention ice cream?"

"Ice c'eam!" Arlo repeated.

"I like a kid with his priorities straight," my mom said.

Kendall smiled. "My treat if you'd like to come along."

"Why not, if Lucy's up for it?" my mother said. "We've got no place special to be."

CHAPTER THIRTY-SEVEN

Lucy

I got in the car with Kendall and the kids to help her out. My mom followed in her car behind us. We went to that store on Santa Monica where they use frozen gas to make the ice cream right before your eyes. Arlo, Mia, and Levi were fascinated by all the blowing vapor. It was like a mad scientist's lab in a movie.

Mom chose blue velvet, which has cupcake chunks in it. I got papaya. Levi, who had strawberry, took two steps out the door, stumbled, and tipped it onto the concrete.

"Uh-oh." He looked up at his mom, chin quivering like he was going to cry.

Kendall didn't blink, just reversed course and steered him back inside.

"Should we take something back to Nana?" I asked my mom while we waited. The sidewalk was busy, and the boulevard was clogged with cars as usual. Across the street was a massive billboard for a new pirate movie with a skull and crossbones and bodies and blood. It was creepy enough to bother me; I hoped the kids did not look up.

"No," my mom said. "If she wants ice cream, she can come and buy it herself."

"Am I going to get to see my father?" I asked. Then I noticed Levi had wandered off to inspect ants emerging from a crack in the sidewalk. People had to change course to get around his squatting body. "Levi! Come back here, please!"

"Ants are hungry," Levi called. He was feeding them

drips of ice cream. Soon someone staring at their phone would walk right into him.

Mia said, "I go get 'im" and took off, dodging around the grown-ups' legs.

"No, Mia, wait!" I called, but she didn't.

My mom, meanwhile, was laughing. "I'd forgotten how much work kids are."

"Unh-hunh," I said as I chased the kids down, rounded them up, juggled their ice cream and mine— while at the same time my brain considered this whole thing with my father. It seemed weird he had come to my game and left and never even said hi.

"Am I going to get to see my father?" I repeated, once Mia and Levi were corralled at an outside table.

My mom licked her ice cream and bit her cone and chewed. "Probably," she said. "He got a place nearby in the Hollywood Hills. He's hoping you want to move there too."

I thought I hadn't heard right, and anyway here came Kendall and Arlo back out of the store. When Levi and Mia saw them, they demanded their own new ice cream.

"Not fair!" they insisted.

"Like so many things," Kendall told them. "Now eat up, and then we'll move out. Nice to see you again, KK."

"Nice to see you, I'm sure, and thank you for the ice cream. It's delish," my mother said.

I sucked in a breath and tried not to cringe. Who says "delish" anyway?

I helped Kendall strap her kids in the car, promised the triplets I would see them soon, then climbed in our own car with my mom. I had lots of questions, but my mom was not much help.

"You'll have to talk to *him*," she said three times in a row. (I counted.) And when I asked when that would be, she said (twice), "He said he'll call."

"Are you getting back together?" I asked. "What about Nana?"

"Nana has nothing to do with it," Mom said. "And good golly, *no*. I am done with that part of my life."

I said, "Oh," feeling stung. What did she mean by that? *I* had come from that part of her life.

At home, Mom parked in the driveway, and we went in

the front door. On the table in the hall with the mail was a package, which I almost didn't see. That's how gloomy our house is. Nana keeps the drapes closed so neighbors can't look in and the lights off to save electricity.

I grabbed the package, which was—*yes!*—just the right size and weight to be cookies. It was too soon for them to be from Olivia, so they must be from Hannah. Olivia's letter had said Hannah sent her, Grace, and Emma cookies. Hooray—my turn at last!

I got a knife in the kitchen, slit the tape, and opened the box. The smell was cinnamon-ginger spicy—*yum!* Sure, I had just eaten an ice cream cone, but I had also just played sixty minutes of soccer. I could definitely manage a cookie. Also, being from Hannah, they would be delicious.

My mother came into the kitchen a few minutes later and sniffed. "What is that heavenly smell? Oh . . . cookies! Are they from your little friends at camp?"

"They're from my counselor, I think. Only—" I had taken a bite by this time, and the taste did not live up to the smell—"they're way underbaked. Doughy instead of chewy, and a couple of days in the mail didn't help. It's weird, though." I held the disappointing cookie up for inspection. "It's not like Hannah to make a baking mistake."

"Does Hannah live in Pennsylvania?" My mom had picked up the box.

"She lives someplace east," I said. "New York?"

"Well, these came from State College, Pennsylvania," my mother said. "The return address says Vivek Sonti. Does that name ring a bell? Or should we call poison control?"

CHAPTER THIRTY-EIGHT

Lucy

Why had Vivek sent me rawish cookies?

I couldn't figure it out.

"I guess I'll throw them away," I told my mother.

"No, don't. That's wasteful," Mom said. "How about freeze them, and I'll ask the pastry chef at the restaurant if she has a suggestion. Speaking of which, I'd better get going."

My mom's current job is waiting tables at a nice

restaurant over on La Cienega. She gets good tips there, too. Nana and I cross our fingers it will work out. I pulled a Ziploc from a drawer, put the cookies inside, then put them in the freezer. It wasn't any more trouble than throwing them away, but I suspected they would still be there at Christmas. Sometimes our freezer is the zone of no return.

Next up: Nana's and my dinner. On the menu that night was fried rice. How you do it is fry leftover rice with frozen vegetables, crack two eggs on top, scramble it all together, sprinkle generously with soy sauce, add one handful roasted peanuts, serve in bowls.

For authenticity, you can eat this with chopsticks. My mother says chopsticks also make you eat slower so you keep your figure. My mother often says this kind of thing. When Nana hears her, she rolls her eyes.

"Did you win your soccer game?" Nana asked when we were settled at the kitchen counter.

"They're the best team in the league," I said. "We lost four to one."

"Don't make excuses," Nana said.

"I scored a goal," I said.

"Too bad no one else did," Nana said.

"What did you do today?" I asked.

"Read some, wrote some," Nana said.

I already knew what she was reading. She likes old novels by Charles Dickens. We have talked about them so much I even know the plots. So I asked, "What did you write about?" not really expecting an answer. My nana is very private.

"This and that," she said. "You a little bit."

"Me?" I had never thought I might appear in Nana's journal. I guessed I thought she wrote about what she was reading. "What did you say about me?" I asked, then added—because I wasn't sure I wanted to know—"You don't have to tell me if you don't want to."

Nana laughed—a sound like a small dog barking. "Today I think I said something about how, against all genetic odds, you are turning into quite a wise and responsible person."

If I was surprised before, I was really surprised now. She had written something nice? "Oh! Uh . . . thank you."

"Don't let it go to your head," Nana said.

For a few minutes after that we chased down rice grains and snow peas in silence. I grabbed the last peanut with my fingers, then asked, "Did Mom tell you she's seen my father?"

Nana didn't answer directly. "I suppose it was inevitable. The rooster comes home to roost."

"He has some big plan," I told her, "something to make money."

"I hope this time it's legal," Nana said.

"Don't you think he's learned his lesson?" I imagined prison as one long time-out. Three years of thinking about what you've done would make anyone behave better, wouldn't it?

"He's never apologized," Nana said. "And the older I get, the more I wonder if any of us ever learns our lesson. What do you think, Lucy?"

"What do I think?" I repeated because I hadn't been listening. Instead, I had been picturing my dad in a small chair in a corner. He looked uncomfortable. Answering my grandmother's question required a brain reset. "Uh, I hope so, I guess. Otherwise what's the point of lessons?"

Nana laughed again. Twice in one dinner—amazing! Then she said she was feeling a little peaked, one of her favorite words, and she thought she'd turn in early. "Thank you for dinner, Lucy. Maybe next time not quite so much soy sauce? It's hard on blood pressure, you know."

"I'll remember," I said, but the truth is I can't win with Nana and soy sauce. When I use less, she asks for the bottle and pours it on.

While I cleared the dishes and washed up, the day's news flashed in my brain: My dad's new place in the hills. My nana writing about me. My mother done with that part of her life. Vivek sending cookies.

CHAPTER THIRTY-NINE

Lucy

People say I'm absentminded, but the truth is more like the opposite: My mind is so present it distracts me from what's going on outside of it.

What happened with the note from Vivek is an example. My brain at once got very busy speculating about why Vivek had sent me cookies—so busy that it never thought to look for the letter in the package that would explain.

And there was one!

It was only luck I saw it. We had a lot of recycling that week, and the next morning the flattened cardboard box fell off the top of the bin as I was carrying it to the curb. I picked the cardboard up from the driveway, and out slipped an envelope labeled LUCY.

I didn't have time to open it then. Clarissa's mom— my ride to school—had just pulled up. I zipped the envelope into a pocket of my backpack and resolved to remember it was there so I could read it during homeroom.

Long story short, I forgot until that night at bedtime.

Monday, May 8

Dear Lucy,

I hope this finds you well. I hope your family is also well.

Thank you for sending the pictures the triplets drew to welcome Anaya to this world. They remain on display on the refrigerator door in our kitchen, and sometimes I point them out to her. I believe the triplet named Levi is an especially talented artist.

I am sorry it has taken me so long to write to you, but it is very hard work being a big brother. (It is probably also hard work being a big sister, but I will never know this from personal experience.)

It seems your babysitting has given you a special interest in children. I have a special interest in them myself now, which has come about from watching Anaya grow from helpless, drowsy infant into someone who can roll over, laugh, babble, and find her toes. As I look back, it happened very quickly. Soon, according to the baby books I have read, she will be creeping, then in short order crawling, walking, and talking.

After that, she goes straight to university. (Hahaha!)

You will have noticed that I also sent cookies.

I suppose it is not allowed for boys to join your "secret cookie club," but the idea of exchanging cookies with friends is sweet (hahaha! That is a play on words!), and so I thought you would not mind receiving some.

Are you looking forward to camp? I will miss Anaya a lot, but it will be good to see my friends (like you?) again.

Yours very sincerely,
Vivek Sonti

P.S. I have printed out a photograph of Anaya and enclosed it.

The photo was still in the envelope. I took it out and studied it, glad I hadn't recycled Vivek's envelope after all. Anaya was a round-faced, round-eyed baby with lots of black hair. In the picture, she was lying on her tummy and staring directly at the camera with a half smile. She seemed sure of herself, as if brotherly attention gives a baby confidence.

I skimmed the letter one more time and thought back to the day Arlo, Mia, and Levi drew the pictures for Baby Anaya. I didn't remember it very well, but it looked like I had managed to mail them. Score one for Lucy! Not so absentminded after all, right? Had I asked Grace for the address? Probably.

And speaking of Grace—did she tell Vivek about the cookie club? Everyone knew she had had a crush on him and then at camp last summer for about two days they were a couple. It made sense she might have told him then, but I felt a little annoyed. *Secret,* right?

I tried to be fair and not mad, though. It's possible I've told secrets before, too, since who can possibly keep track of what's secret and what's not? Also, each of us—Grace, Olivia, Emma, and me—sent Vivek anonymous cookies last year as a joke. For a boy, he is an okay kid, even if his cookies are bad.

The next morning I used a magnet with the phone number for takeout pizza to stick the picture of Anaya on our refrigerator. My mother wouldn't notice, but

Nana probably would. It would give us something to talk about at dinner.

It was 7:43—seven minutes till my ride came, plenty of time for breakfast. Also, for once, the milk wasn't sour. I was pouring Special K into a bowl when my mom appeared in the doorway.

"Good morning, honeybun," she said, yawning. She was wearing the ratty red-and-gold USC T-shirt she sleeps in. Her blond hair was a tangle, and her eye makeup was smudged.

"What are you doing up?" I asked. My mom works late and usually goes out afterward. She is never awake when I leave for school.

"Your dad"—she yawned again—"is picking you up today."

"What? He can't. I mean, Clarissa's mom gives me a ride home from school. What are you talking about?"

"Not today," Mom said. "Your dad wants to talk to you. You can go out for an early dinner or something maybe."

"No, we can't," I said. "What will Nana do?"

"Nana can heat up something," Mom said. "Don't you want to see your dad?"

What I wanted was breakfast. So I didn't answer, just wolfed cereal and then put the milk away. Now it was 7:49, and I had to go.

"Dad's not on the approved list at school." I shouldered my backpack and headed for the door. "The office won't let kids go with just anybody. As far as they know, Dad doesn't exist. He can't pick me up."

End of discussion, right? That's what I thought, and a second later, I was in the driveway, but—OMG— Mom followed me out the door, ratty T-shirt, tangles, smudges, and all.

"Wait, Lucy! I'll call the school. You get out at three ten, right? Or three fifteen? Oh, hi, Clarissa—nice to see you. Hi, Clarissa's mom. Thanks for driving!"

I have been my mother's daughter for my whole life, and it takes a lot to embarrass me—but this was embarrassing. Luckily, Clarissa's mom seemed to understand. "Good morning, KK! Have a good day!"

She waved to my mom and drove off as soon as the car door slammed. I did not look back.

Clarissa likes to ride in the backseat and pretend her mom is a chauffeur. Now she looked over at me with wide eyes and blinked. "Lucy, is your mom okay? She seemed a little crazy!"

"*Clarissa!*" Her mother glared at her in the rearview mirror.

"Well, she did," Clarissa said. "I'm just concerned is all, because I'm a caring human. Is she okay, Lucy?"

This was a rare moment when my ditzy reputation came in handy. "Why wouldn't she be?" I said, which is a tough question to answer—right?—tough enough to stump Clarissa.

It's a short ride to school, and Clarissa's mom filled the silence with a stream of comments: "It's pretty warm today," "That math homework was hard," and "The PTA raised a bundle with the produce sale."

When we pulled up by the main entrance, Clarissa climbed out—"Have a good day, honey!"—and her mom twisted around to look at me. "Lucy, you need a ride home, right? Seriously, is everything okay? I don't want to leave you in the lurch."

"Yes. Kind of. What's a lurch?" I said.

"It means, uh . . . a pickle, I guess? Off-balance."

I pictured myself teetering on one toe and thought that was about right. Still, I didn't want Clarissa's mom to worry. "I'll be fine, I think. Thanks for being nice."

"Anytime, Lucy. See you at three o'clock."

CHAPTER FORTY

Lucy

Here are some things my teachers talked about in school
that day: Father Junipero Serra, sedimentary rock, number lines.

If any of it was important, I have catching up to do.

Instead of listening, I was looking out the window
at sparrows in the trees and seagulls in the dull gray
sky. I was thinking about my father. What I knew about
him was what I had pieced together from my mom and

Nana and Aunt Freda. He is charming, funny, and smart, they agree. He is unreliable and late a lot. Sometimes he loses his temper.

None of that answered the Big Question, though, the one I had wondered ever since I was old enough to understand that I had a father I didn't know. It looked like soon I was going to have a chance to ask it, but I would need to summon up some bravery first. I would need what Olivia calls "gumption."

School ends at three. A little before that, I was looking out the computer-lab window when a messenger opened the door and said, "Excuse me? Can Lucy Ambrose come to the office, please?"

The teacher, Mrs. Hamilton, had been helping my friend Emmaline. Now she straightened up and looked first at me, then at the messenger. "Should she take her backpack so she's ready for dismissal?"

The messenger was a fourth-grade boy whose name I couldn't remember. You could tell the job made him feel important. "Yes," he said. "She should."

Emmaline shot me a look that meant, *Is everything*

okay? I shrugged because I didn't know. Then I got my backpack and followed the fourth grader out the door. Maybe it's different at your school, but at mine older kids and younger kids don't talk to each other. It would have been majorly strange if either of us had said a word as we walked.

In the office, a man was standing by the counter, while the two secretaries were laughing at something he had said. Even though the man had been on my mind all day, I didn't recognize him for a couple of seconds, and when I did, I got a shock. He looked so much older than he did in pictures, more wrinkled, and his hair was gray. He dressed the same as ever, though—classic, my mom would have said: nice jeans, a turquoise polo shirt, and loafers.

I must not have looked the same as my pictures either, because when I came in, he glanced down and then away. For a moment, I knew him but he didn't know me.

Then Mrs. Franklin spoke. She's the principal's secretary. "Here's Lucy now," she said. "And Lucy, here's your father. Your mother okayed him for the approved list, so it's all copacetic on our side. Are you good?"

I was amazed to see my father right here in front of me after so much time, and almost equally amazed that my mom had actually called the school. I didn't answer right away. Mrs. Franklin waited patiently. I have gone to this school since kindergarten. Finally, she said, "Earth to Lucy?"

"Good," I said, more or less remembering the question.

"Good," she said. "It's near enough to three o'clock that you can take her, Mr. Ambrose."

"Call me Cary," my father said.

"Righty-o," said Mrs. Franklin. "Have a nice evening, now. So very nice to meet you."

"Shall we?" Now my father looked me in the eye and smiled. He didn't seem a bit embarrassed that five seconds ago he had no idea who I was. "I can carry that backpack for you."

"I'm used to it," I said.

Outside I saw the parents in cars waiting at the curb and thought of Clarissa's mom. "Do you have a phone?" I asked my father.

"Who doesn't?" he said.

"Me," I said. "Can I borrow it a sec? I'll give it back."

Because our landline at home is ancient, I've actually memorized people's phone numbers. Most of the time this wastes brain storage, but at that moment, it was useful.

"*Who* do I know in the seven-eight-six area code??" Clarissa's mom said when she picked up.

"It's Lucy," I said. "Lucy's father, I mean—*my* father. I'm Lucy."

"Lucy! Are you all right? I'm just turning in to the school drive now."

"I'm fine. My dad's picking me up. That's why I have his phone."

There was a pause. Then Clarissa's mom said, "Yes, I see you and your dad. Hang on. Let me park. I'd like to say hello."

"Wait. What's happening?" my father asked when I handed him back the phone.

"Clarissa's mom," I said, and a moment later I saw her striding across the parking lot, waving, a brilliant smile on her face.

There were the usual nice-to-meet-you's. My dad said, "Call me Cary." Clarissa's mom said, "I'm Emily."

"Pretty name," said my father. "And how do you know Lucy?"

"I'm a neighbor," said Clarissa's mom, "and a friend. Your daughter has many, many friends, and we all think she is a lovely young woman."

My father looked down at me and smiled. "Of course she is," he said.

Meanwhile, I felt embarrassed and kind of confused by the attention.

"And all of us look out for her," Clarissa's mom continued. She wasn't smiling anymore. Standing very straight, she was almost as tall as my father.

"Very kind," said my father.

"I wouldn't call it kindness, per se," said Clarissa's mom. "It's more because of how much we value and appreciate her. And I expect that you do too. Am I right, Cary?"

"Yes." My father took a half step back. "Yes, of course."

"Well, that is excellent, then," said Clarissa's mom.

"And now I'd better find my own daughter and take her home. Piano lessons today." Smiling again, she looked down at me. "I'll see you in the morning, Lucy."

"See you in the morning," I said.

I had the feeling something had just happened, but I wasn't sure what.

As for my father, I guess he thought something had just happened too. "Formidable woman," he said.

CHAPTER FORTY-ONE

Lucy

What does a kid do with her father anyway? How would I even know? How would he? My dad's car was a blue Mercedes—a rental, he told me—and for a few minutes we made right and left turns on the streets around my school, going nowhere slow.

My father suggested pizza. My father suggested ice cream. I politely declined both, saying I'd had a big lunch, but the truth was I felt too nervous to eat.

"Shopping?" my father said. "A new party dress? Do girls wear party dresses?"

"No," I said.

"Wait—I know," my father said. "I believe I heard from a little bird that you are a good artist like your mother is. In fact, I think you won an award for art last year, didn't you?"

"Do birds talk to you?" I asked.

My father laughed and pulled a U-turn in the middle of a block. "I know the perfect place," he said, and soon we were on Wilshire, heading toward downtown.

"The art museum," I guessed.

My father nodded. "So you got my sense of direction and not your mother's," he said.

"Mom's is okay," I said.

"Oh?" My father glanced over at me. "Then how did she manage to get lost on a cruise ship where all the decks are labeled and all the cabins, too? It is nearly impossible to get lost on a cruise ship."

"You were on a cruise ship with Mom?" I said.

"Lots of times," he said. "I guess she doesn't talk about that time in her life, does she?"

"Not really," I said.

My father found a parking spot on a street near the museum. We got out and walked around palm trees and the grove of old city streetlights to the entrance. "Shall we buy tickets?" my father asked. "Or just sit and admire the sculpture and chat?"

At that moment I wished even more than before that I was in the car with Clarissa's mom. What was I supposed to answer? My mom and grandmother never have money. Same with my father? Was that why he wasn't buying us tickets?

But he was driving an expensive car.

My dad's smile flickered. "Really," he said, "either one is fine."

"I was just here on a field trip," I said.

"So let's hang, then." He gestured toward a bench, and we sat down. "The point is to get to know each other, right? And it's a nice day. For weather, you can't beat Southern California."

If you're wondering, I did not ask my Big Question—not that afternoon. My father did most of the talking. He told me his big plan "involved finance," but he had to "overcome certain regulatory hurdles" before he could "bring it to fruition."

He showed me photos of the house in the Hollywood Hills on his phone. It was not a mansion or anything, just a cute normal house with three bedrooms—one for me, and my own bathroom—and lots of windows. It had a pool. He told me he didn't own it yet, but it was "under contract" and I could take a tour in person soon.

When I asked, he said he had missed seeing me kick the goal, but he would have plenty more chances to come to my games.

After a while the bench got hard. "I have homework," I said.

"And you've got to be hungry by now, right?" He stood up.

"We could get fast food," I said. "I could take something to Nana. Otherwise she might not eat."

"Done," he said, "but I'll drop you off if you don't mind. I'm not so popular with Nana."

We picked up burgers from the drive-through at In-N-Out and ate French fries as we drove. Two blocks from my house, my father looked at me and asked, "So what do you say?"

"Thank you," I said—which made him laugh.

"That's not what I meant. What I'm asking is do you want to come and live with me when the sale goes through? The house is plenty big, and I'll work it so you stay at your school. You can have a phone of your own like normal kids, and a laptop, too."

"What about the triplets? Do you know about the triplets?" I said.

"The kids you watch? There's no shortage of babysitters, Lucy."

We were on my street by this time. My father pulled into the driveway. I put my hand on the door latch. "Thank you for the food."

"You are welcome." My father grinned. His teeth were straight and very white. "And you think about my offer, okay? I talked to your mom already, and you can see her as much as you want to. The new place is not even a freeway away."

I had barely pushed the front door open when my grandmother called from her bedroom, "Lucy? Where have you been?"

OMG—hadn't my mother told her?

"I've got food," I answered. "Come in the kitchen and eat."

CHAPTER FORTY-TWO

Lucy

Nana must have been surprised that dinner was fast food. She must have wondered where it had come from and where I had been.

She didn't ask, though. She might've been distracted by the French fries, which are her favorite, even though by the time we ate them they were cooling off and limp. I didn't volunteer any information. I didn't want to get into it about my dad. What would be the point?

I did not see my mom either that night or the next morning. Not unusual. In the car going to school, Clarissa's mom—Emily—asked how my father and I had gotten along, and Clarissa said, "Father? But I thought you didn't have a father."

We were stopped at a stop sign. Clarissa's mom did the glare-in-the-rearview-mirror thing and started to speak, but I spoke first. "Everyone has a father. Mammals anyway. We learned it in science, remember?"

"But you're—," Clarissa began.

"—also a mammal," I said, then, "It was okay," to her mom's reflection in the rearview mirror. "Thanks for, uh . . ." I thought back to the afternoon before, the way Clarissa's mom had talked to my father. I didn't know how to describe what had happened.

"For caring?" Clarissa's mom suggested.

"Yeah," I said.

When I got home that day, there was a package for me on the hall table and a letter, too. The package was from O, and so was the letter—forwarded by Hannah.

It was a Friday, and Coach Kamae had brought me home. We'd had an away game, and we had won, but none of my fans had been there.

There were a few minutes before I needed to make dinner, so I went to my room, kicked off my cleats, set the package on my desk, and dropped back onto my bed. I would give my tired legs a rest while reading Olivia's letter. On the back of the envelope was a handwritten note from Hannah.

Hi, Lucy—

Apparently, Olivia mailed this letter to me by mistake. When you read it, you will understand that I am feeling pretty angry at you Flowerpot girls. I am committed to Moonlight Ranch this summer, but it might be best if you four had a different counselor.

One other thing: I had intended to send you cookies this
semester, but Travis liked my cookies so much I didn't have
time to bake for you (or anybody else but Travis). Sorry about
that. Good luck with the rest of your school year.

—Hannah

OMG.

A new counselor?! *What had happened?* Why was
Hannah mad?

I tore open the envelope so fast I almost ripped the
inside letter in two. I read it fast as well . . . and then I
was mad at Olivia.

Why had she said all that stuff about piecing
together Travis's breakup letter and sneaking cookies
to Lance? And why had she been so careless about
the two envelopes?

I couldn't imagine Moonlight Ranch if I wasn't
in Flowerpot Cabin with Grace, Emma, Olivia, *and*
Hannah.

I had one more letter from Olivia to read, the one I knew I would find enclosed in the package. There was nothing it could say to make me feel better, but there was one consoling thought: cookies.

Using the scissors from my desk drawer, I opened the box, unfolded sheets of wax paper, and found beneath dozens of small, plain, perfect discs that smelled like butter and sugar—shortbread. Without even thinking, I ate two. They were an excellent aid to tired-muscle recovery. I felt not quite so angry at Olivia too.

She had never expected Hannah to read that stuff, after all—and yeah, she had been careless, but everybody is sometimes. Who was it that hadn't even gotten around to forwarding Olivia's old thank-you note to Hannah?

That would be me.

This letter, like the other one, was handwritten on Olivia's own cream-colored stationery. OLIVIA!!!! it said in all caps at the top. There was only one sheet.

May 9, Tuesday

Greetings to the most perfectly Lucy Lucy that I know.

I wish wish WISH I had the leisure to write you a long long LONG letter, but—alas and alack—I do not. Tonight is the final performance of <u>Little Red Riding Hood</u> at After-School Acting Studio, and Second Chipmunk (a minor character) has to be backstage to attach ears to hair, whiskers to face, and costume to self one full hour before curtain time.

Jenny and I made these cookies today after school. We chose an easy, fast recipe because IMHO it is IMPERATIVE that you receive your dosage of flour power AS SOON AS POSSIBLE under the circumstances!!!!

These cookies have been specially formulated to help you face your father because fathers are something I happen to know something about. Here is the 411 on the subject: Fathers are always giving their kids advice, which is really just their sneaky way of telling kids what to do.

And this is the important part, Lucy—please try to pay attention!!!!

As a kid, it is your absolute responsibility to fight back the way my brother, Troy, did when he quit baseball. Probably fathers actually do know something sometimes, but not as often as they think they do, and it is your one and only life, and you must live it yourself—just as I must live mine, and Troy must live his, and—according to my acting teacher, Mrs. Wanderling—Second Chipmunk must live hers, which is personal and distinctive and important.

While it is true Second Chipmunk only has one line, the line is key to the action, and this is it: "Go that way, little girl!"

I deliver it with so much AUTHORITY, if I do

say so myself, that Esmee Snyder has no choice but to obey.

Still seven more weeks till camp! How will we survive??? Love you always, dear dear Lucy and best to your father too—Cheers from O, the most exalted and loudest Second Chipmunk in theater history!!!

CHAPTER FORTY-THREE

Lucy

That night I dreamed about a forest straight out of *Bambi*, which at the moment was tied with *SpongeBob* at the top of the triplets' playlist. I always think the part with the mother at the beginning is too sad for children, but Arlo, Mia, and Levi barely notice. They are more interested in twitterpated rabbits singing songs.

In my dream, a rock splashed into a blue pool, and

the fish freaked out and the frogs dove off their lily pads.

There was other stuff, too, the way there always is in dreams—cookies, broken flowerpots, a dark-haired baby, a hunter with white teeth, a chipmunk yelling at a little girl in a ratty red T-shirt. None of it fit together.

I told Kendall about my dream the next morning when I went over to their house to watch the triplets. Their family lives in a new house at the end of our cul-de-sac. When I got there, the triplets' dad was home with them watching cartoons, but he had to leave to go to work, and Kendall was taking Piper to infant water orientation at the Y.

"Was your dream a nightmare?" Kendall asked. We were in the kitchen, and she was collecting the equipment she needed to walk out the door with Piper. "Mia's been having nightmares. You know how sometimes she's hard to understand? Twice she woke up crying about a *pie-ott*, or maybe *pie-itt*?"

"Poor Mia," I said.

Kendall took a breath and looked around. "Okay,"

she said, then scooped up baby, baby seat, and diaper bag. "We should be home in an hour, give or take."

I said, "See you soon," then remembered something and pulled a letter from my pocket. "Can you mail this for me?" I had finally resealed Olivia's thank-you note, crossed out my address, written Hannah's on it, and added a new stamp.

"Sure thing," said Kendall. "I go right by the post office. I think it will go out today."

Piper was sound asleep in her car seat when Kendall returned. "There is nothing like swimming to tire a baby out—*oh!*" She had come into the family room to find Arlo, Levi, Mia, and me dressed up in hats, old scarves, and costume jewelry. Levi had a black patch on one eye.

"Ahoy there!" Arlo greeted his mom.

"Ahoy back." Kendall grinned. "Are we playing pirates?"

"Yo ho ho and a bottle of rum!" Mia had found one of Piper's bottles and now raised it over her head.

"I figured out Mia was saying pirate," I explained.

"The—you know—*nightmares*?" I whispered the last word.

Kendall nodded. "Oh, now it makes sense—sort of."

"She saw a billboard by the ice cream store," I said.

"Pipah walk da pank!" Levi waved a pool noodle in Piper's general direction.

"Levi, she can't walk at all yet," I said.

"Mommy walk da pank!" Levi waved the pool noodle at Kendall—who held her arms up and acted terrified until Levi started to giggle.

"No pirates in Beverly Hills, Mommy," Mia said solemnly. "Only us."

"Is that what Lucy told you?" Kendall said. "She's absolutely right."

"No more bad dreams," said Mia.

"Good!" Kendall said. "What would we do without Lucy?"

I stayed over for lunch and read to the triplets before they went down for naps. On my way to leave, I found Kendall nursing Piper in the living room.

"Thanks a bazillion," Kendall said. "Oh—and I've

been meaning to ask what's up with your father. Have you gotten a chance to see him?"

"We went to the art museum—*outside* the art museum, anyway. He bought burgers," I said.

Kendall nodded. "So that's nice. I mean, was it nice? Are you going to see him again?"

"It was strange," I said.

Kendall looked down at Piper. "You have to get used to each other," she said.

"Do we?" I said.

Kendall looked up at me and blinked. "I mean, if you want to. Do you want to?"

"I don't know," I said. "Sometimes I wish someone would tell me what to do. Isn't that what grown-ups are for? Isn't that what parents are for?"

Kendall seemed ready to answer, but Piper was fussy. "Ohhh, little baby," Kendall cooed. "Do you need a change? Do you need a nap? What can I do for you?"

"I gotta go." I started toward the door. "See you next week, Kendall."

"Righty-o, Lucy," Kendall said. "I'm sure things will all work out."

It was a little after one when I got home. My mom was awake, wearing normal clothes, and standing in the kitchen. "There you are at last, Lucy," she said. "Let's make a cheesecake. Want to?"

I was amazed. "Why?"

My mom giggled. "All those bad cookies in the freezer, right? I asked the pastry chef what to do with them, and that was her suggestion. Cookie crust for a cheesecake."

"You remembered to ask the pastry chef?"

"I did. I also picked up the ingredients on my way home from work last night." Mom sounded very proud of herself.

"What's gotten into you?" I said.

Mom ignored this question. "The pastry chef printed the recipe out when I told her we didn't have a computer. She gave me a pretty funny look, but here it is." She held up a sheet of paper, and I read it over.

MARTHA FREEMAN

"We can't make this," I announced. "We don't have a food processor."

"Oh, for heaven's sake." Mom rolled her eyes. "There weren't always food processors, you know. We can crush the cookies with a rolling pin between sheets of wax paper. That's how we did it in home ec. I didn't grow up in a fancy school district like this one, you know. We had to make do."

"You took home ec?" I said.

"It was harder than you'd think," Mom said. "We have a rolling pin, don't we?"

"When was the last time you followed a recipe?" I asked. "Do you even know what's in this kitchen?"

"Nope," Mom said cheerily. "But I am fixin' to find out."

The cheesecake project did not start well. My mom and I had very different ideas on how to proceed. For example, she did not believe in using the microwave to melt butter or soften cream cheese. She believed the microwave gave off dangerous radiation.

"You sound like Nana when she talks about

screens," I said. "They use microwaves at the restaurant, right?"

"Precisely!" she said. "And that's why I don't need additional wave thingies"—she raised her fingers and wiggled them ominously—"cavorting among my delicate brain cells."

"Okay, fine," I said. "We can melt the butter in a saucepan and cut up the cream cheese in cubes. By the time we're ready, it will be soft enough."

"Good thinking, Lucy," my mom said. "Now you deal with the cookies, and I will address myself to these eggs. Hey, Humpty Dumpty?" She held one up. "Fallen from any walls lately?"

"You're weird, Mom," I said.

It's true I could have made a bakery's worth of cheesecakes in the time it took my mom and me to make one. Still, with her stupid jokes and good mood, it was kind of fun. We don't do stuff together that much. Our schedules aren't the same, and anyway, she's embarrassing. With no one else around, I wasn't embarrassed.

As the cheesecake baked, the kitchen filled with its aroma, spicy like Vivek's bad cookies but toasty and cream cheesy, too.

"I'll get plates," Mom announced when the timer rang.

"We can't eat it yet," I said. "It has to cool. If we cut it now, it'll be goo."

"You're kidding," said Mom, "and how do you know that anyway?"

"Cooking shows," I said.

Mom sighed. "So be that way," she said, as if the cooling time of cheesecakes were my fault. "I guess I'll just have to get my piece for breakfast. Now, I need to get ready for work. Look, Lucy, there's one other thing before I take off. That was fun, right?"

"Yeah, sure," I said, putting the potholders away and turning off the oven. What would I make Nana for dinner? I hoped Mom wouldn't mind if I gave Nana a piece of cheesecake for dessert. She hadn't come out of her room to see what was going on, but she had to have smelled it baking.

"So when you come back to visit," Mom said, "we can do stuff. We can cook together, or I'll come to your soccer games more. It'll be good, right? I'll be fine."

As is usual with me, the words didn't make sense right away. When they did, I spun around to look at her. "What? What are you talking about?"

"When you go to live with your father—your dad, I mean," she said. "It's a better opportunity for you. You can have a normal life with a phone—more like the way your friends live."

"You want me to go?" My knees felt wobbly.

"Other kids go on family vacations to Disney and get takeout Chinese whenever they want," Mom said. "Other kids don't have to make dinner. You should live like that, too, and this is your chance."

"What if I don't want to?" The barstools were behind me, and I sat down. Mom was in the middle of the kitchen, her hands on her hips. She was leaning toward me slightly.

"Of course you want to," she said. "What kid

wouldn't want to? He's gonna have a swimming pool."

Thinking of the pool made me think of my dream. Mom must've been thinking, too, because all of a sudden, she giggled.

"What?" I said, annoyed.

"You look *so* serious, Lucy. You used to make that face when you were a baby. I remember one time . . ."

"When?" I said.

"It was the day you found your toes," Mom said. "You know how babies' eyes aren't focused at first? And then gradually the world comes into view. Anyway, I guess to you those toes appeared out of nowhere, and your face showed deep, deep concern— like, 'OMG, what have we here? Are they mine? Are they dangerous?'"

I shook my head and couldn't help but smile. "So back then you could read my mind?"

"Sometimes I could, not always," she said. "I wish I could do it now."

"Do you want me to go live with Dad?" I asked. There. The question was out and could not be taken back.

"No," Mom said. "That is, yes. I don't know. I want what's best for you."

"Okay," I said.

"Okay . . . what?"

"Okay, I'm going to think about it."

CHAPTER FORTY-FOUR

Lucy

I had one more question, the Big One for my father.

I got my chance to ask it the next day, Sunday.

He had phoned after my mom left for work Saturday night—while Nana and I were eating dinner. I picked up because Nana hates to talk on the phone.

"Hey, Lu, I got the keys to the house!" he said. "I'll come and get you tomorrow—what do you say?"

"Do you own it now?" I asked him.

"Still some paperwork to do," he said. "But nobody's in it, so we can stop by. Ten a.m.? Or do you prefer to sleep in like your mom?"

"Ten is fine," I said.

Dad pulled into the driveway and honked at 10:05 the next morning. I was waiting by the front door, holding a tin of Olivia's cookies. "Bye, Nana!" I called. My hand was on the doorknob when she spoke up behind me.

"I should come out and say hello to your father."

"What?" I turned and saw her standing in the door-way between the hall and the kitchen. She wore jeans and a Bob Marley T-shirt. Her gray hair was pulled back in a tight bun. She was barefoot. "No, no—you don't have to do that," I said.

"It's the courteous thing to do," she said. Then she walked right past me and opened the door.

Oh no.

My father must've jumped out of the car the second

he saw her. By the time I got outside, he was walking briskly up the driveway. His smile was so big that his cheeks must have hurt. "Mrs. Jessup," he said. "Very nice to see you, an unexpected pleasure."

"I'll bet," said Nana, backing away from a hug. "You've gone gray, I see. And the car must've set you back some pennies."

"It's a rental," I said.

Nana looked at me, then at my father. "Who is it you're trying to impress?" she asked.

"Straight-shooting as ever, Mrs. Jessup. I guess I got used to a certain style of living once upon a time, and I hope to get used to it again," he said.

"And just how do you plan to pull that off?" Nana said. "If you don't mind my asking."

"The details would take a while to explain," my father said.

"Go ahead," said Nana. "I have no pressing business just at the moment."

"Well, the thing is, you see, that I do," my father said. "After Lucy and I take a look at the house, I've got some meetings set up. My time's not my own. You know how it is."

"I don't, actually," Nana said. "But I'll take your word for it. Lucy, dear, are you okay? I'll see you back here soon it sounds like."

"I'm fine, Nana," I said.

"All right, then, my dear." Nana put her hand on my shoulder. "You and your father carry on."

"Whoa," my father said as soon as we had pulled out of the driveway. "*She* hasn't changed a bit."

When I didn't answer, he asked what kind of music I wanted. I said I didn't care, and he put on classical.

"What's in the tin?" he asked.

I told him a friend had sent me cookies. I didn't mention flour power. "They're shortbread. They're good. Do you want one?"

"Let's wait till we get to the house," he said.

We took Santa Monica to Sunset to Hollywood Boulevard, where the Walk of Fame and Grauman's Chinese Theatre are. Then we wound around a little and hung a left and wound around a lot up into the hills.

Soon my father turned sharply into the driveway of the house I'd seen in the photos, which clung for dear life to the downhill slope. "What if there's an earthquake?" I asked.

"Nothing to worry about." He laughed. "It's come through three big ones with flying colors." My father unlocked the front door, which was orange, and we went inside. There was no furniture, and it was very light, especially compared to Nana's. The walls were pastel colors. There were sliding glass doors out to the pool.

"Can we sit on the edge?" I said. "Can we put our feet in the water?"

My father shrugged. "How 'bout if I come out with you, and you go ahead. I don't want to get my feet wet, though. I don't have a towel to dry them."

It was a warm day, a little smoggy; the water felt good. Beyond the pool, the hills fell away and the flat, hazy city spread out to the coast.

My dad sat down at an angle to me, his legs outstretched. "How about that cookie?" he said.

I opened the tin, and we each took a couple. "Really

excellent," he said after a bite. "You're lucky to have a friend who can bake."

"I can bake too," I said.

He nodded, but I could see his thoughts were somewhere else. "So what do you think?" he said finally. "Have I sold you on the deal? You really can't beat this house, can you?"

"The house is nice," I said. "But can I tell you something? I don't know you that well. I don't even know what to call you. I never had a dad till now."

My father's face clouded. "What do you mean? I've stayed in touch."

"You sent birthday cards," I said.

My father breathed in and out. "Fair enough. But Freda vouches for me, doesn't she? I have your best interests at heart."

Freda is my aunt—my dad's stepsister, the one who pays for camp. "Yeah," I said slowly. "But how much do you care about me?"

That was it. The Big Question. Maybe it was flour power that gave me the courage to ask.

"A lot," my father said.

His eyes were very sincere, but I wasn't done with my questions. "So then where have you been? You got out of prison years ago. You could have seen me anytime. I was right here."

My dad set his mouth in a line, then breathed. "You don't have to bring up prison. A grown-up's life is complicated, Lucy. You'll understand that someday."

"I feel pretty grown-up now," I said.

"I see that," my father said, "and I'm not sure it's right. You should get to be a kid and have fun."

I had thought those things myself, not to mention how I wanted to live in a house that wasn't as dark as a tomb, a house where we didn't always worry about money. And here was my father saying it out loud. Was he the prince in a fairy tale come to my rescue? But if he was, wouldn't I know it for sure?

My father started to laugh. "You are making one heck of a frowny face, Lu," he said. "Watch out or it'll freeze that way. The fact is, I wouldn't presume to tell you what to do."

CHAPTER FORTY-FIVE

P.S.

Sunday, July 2, Moonlight Ranch

After the mix-up with the letters, Hannah had thought hard about whether she wanted to return to her four campers in Flowerpot Cabin. Once finals were over, she phoned her friend Jane, the counselor in Purple Sage, to ask if she'd be willing to switch.

"I don't get you at all," Jane said. "I thought you loved those girls—even if Purple Sage did crush you in the Top Cabin competition last year."

When Hannah explained, Jane laughed and couldn't stop.

"Hey, cut it out. They're a bunch of little sneaks!" Hannah said.

Jane inhaled and controlled herself. "Look at it this way," she said. "Those girls went to a lot of trouble to make you happy. And besides, didn't Olivia call you the undisputed best counselor? So how do I compete with that?"

"Oh, that doesn't mean anything," Hannah said. "It's just how Olivia talks."

"I doubt that," said Jane. "And anyway, it worked out pretty much the way they planned it, right? Last I heard, you didn't like Travis any more than they do."

Privately, Hannah thought this was the most annoying part. The girls had been right about Travis and right about Jack, too. On that day in May, the day before her Renaissance art final, when she got the wrong letter from Olivia, she had phoned Jack in a snit to tell him how her campers had invaded her privacy and plotted to fix her up with another counselor, Lance.

She had expected him to be mad at them too.

But he wasn't. He thought the whole thing was hilarious and that the girls should be commended for recognizing his vast superiority to Travis. The two of them were on the phone a long time.

And so it was Hannah who greeted Grace, Emma, Olivia, and their families on Camper Arrival Day in the parking lot outside the Moonlight Ranch main gate, the same as she had done each of the two summers before.

Lucy was late, as usual.

"Is her mom bringing her again?" Emma asked. It was after lunch. The families had left. The girls were unpacking in Flowerpot Cabin. Buck, the camp director, had imposed the no-electronics rule again, and Olivia swore she was going through phone withdrawal.

"I thought Lucy was moving in with her dad," Olivia said.

Emma shook her head. "I saw Vivek at lunch. Lucy phoned him a couple of weeks ago. She's still with her mom."

"Wait—you saw Vivek at lunch?" Grace said.

"Uh-oh. Here we go," said Olivia.

Grace had been folding her underwear. Now she turned to look at Oliva. "What's that supposed to mean?"

"Hello-o-o?" said Emma. "This is not about Vivek, right? Lucy is living with her mom and her nana, same as before. Her dad wanted her to move in with him, but she decided she didn't want to. He moved to a house near theirs, though, so she sees him more than before."

"And who gets the credit for that one?" Olivia waggled her thumbs at herself. "*Moi*—Olivia Baron! I *warned* her about dads, how they always give orders. I bet he tried to tell her what to do, and she said she was in charge of her own life, thank you very much."

Emma shut the lid of her suitcase and shoved it under her bunk. "Either that or the other way around. Vivek told me Lucy didn't think her father acted the way a dad was supposed to. He didn't seem to know what she should do at all."

Olivia shrugged. "Same thing," she said. "And either way, I get credit."

"Vivek said something about babies and their toes, too," Emma said. "How Lucy's mom turned out to be paying attention just when Lucy least expected it? I didn't quite understand. I was trying to spread mayo on my sandwich, and he just kept talking. Oh—he also showed me a picture of his little sister. What a cutie!"

"Could we be done with Vivek now?" Grace said.

"Looks like someone isn't," Olivia said.

"You must mean Lucy," Grace said.

"And speaking of Lucy," said a voice from the door-way—a voice that turned out to be Lucy's own.

"Hey, you!" Hannah had been filling out paperwork while half listening to her campers' chatter. Now she jumped up from her desk. "Welcome back! Do you need help with your stuff?"

At the same time, Grace, Emma, and Olivia were shrieking "Lucy!" "Lucy!" "Lucy!" and overwhelming their friend with hugs.

"Uh, hi. It's great to be here, you guys." Lucy smiled weakly. "Uh, is lunch over? Is there any food? My mom forgot her credit card, and we drove all the way from—"

"Oh, you poor thing!" There was a general chorus of concern.

"I've got cookies," Hannah said, then laughed. "Of course I do. Uh, Jack sent them to me—like a welcome back to camp. I think he's sorry he's not here."

"Wait, what?" said Olivia.

"Jack?" said Emma.

"Seriously?" said Grace.

"Yes. Jack. Seriously. And I guess I'll explain in a minute. Emma—run and talk to Mrs. Arthur in the kitchen. See if she won't—," Hannah started to say.

"On my way!" Emma tripped out the door.

A few minutes later, Lucy sat at Hannah's desk eating a PB&J while Grace, Emma, and Olivia ate Hannah's chocolate chip cookies.

"Yes, Jack and I are back together," Hannah said. "And yes, you guys were right about Travis. But that doesn't make it okay for you to pry into my personal life. No more of that this summer. Promise?"

"How can we promise? You might need our help," said Emma.

"*Promise*," Hannah repeated.

"Oh, all right. We promise," said Olivia.

"I'm not blind, O. I can see that your fingers are crossed," Hannah said.

"What? My fingers?" Olivia said. "They must have done that on their own."

"Are there any more cookies?" Lucy asked.

"Uh-oh," said Emma. "This might be the last one."

Monday, July 3

Dear Jack,

Greetings from Flowerpot Cabin, and Happy Independence Day!

It was very kind of you to send our beloved counselor, Hannah, a box of chocolate chip cookies to welcome her back to camp. As you know, we residents of Flowerpot Cabin know a thing or two about baking, and we can sincerely opine that your cookies were of the very highest quality.

While we are devastated that you decided to get a real job this summer instead of coming back to camp, we will strive to have a good time anyway, and we also promise to take good care of Hannah. She says she does not want us running her romantic life anymore, but we did get her to admit that so far we have done an awesome job.

Very, very, very, very sincerely!!!!
Olivia, Grace, Emma, and Lucy

P.S. Send more cookies.

Cookie Recipes

Hey, cookie bakers!

Baking is a blast, but make sure you ask an adult for help with the oven or mixer. Have fun!

XX, Hannah

Chocolate Macaroons

(Makes about 36 macaroons)

2 ½ cups dried unsweetened shredded coconut

1 ½ tablespoons potato starch or flour

½ cup sugar

¼ teaspoon salt

4 large egg whites

1 teaspoon vanilla

12 ounces (one bag) chocolate chips, divided

Stir together shredded coconut, potato starch, sugar, and salt till blended. Break up any chunks of potato starch with a fork.

In a smaller bowl, whisk together the egg whites and vanilla till frothy.

Pour the egg white mixture into the dried coconut

mixture. Use a fork to stir the batter together, making sure the coconut is fully and evenly moistened by the egg whites. Let the mixture sit for 20 to 30 minutes while the coconut rehydrates.

Preheat oven to 325°F. Stir the batter again with a fork. Line a baking sheet with parchment paper. Scoop up the batter in tablespoonfuls and drop them onto the baking sheet, evenly spaced. They won't spread, so you can bake them fairly close together.

Bake the macaroons for 20 to 25 minutes till the bottom edges turn golden and the tips of the coconut shreds start to brown. Remove from the oven. Don't overbake or they will become dry. Cool on baking sheet. When cool, first place them on a flat surface lined with parchment paper. Melt 9 ounces chocolate chips, either in the microwave or in a double boiler. I melt mine in the microwave at 50 percent power for 1 minute, stir, then continue to melt in 15-second bursts at 50 percent power till the chocolate becomes smooth.

Grasp each macaroon at the top and dip the wider

base into the melted chocolate, twisting it into the chocolate and coating it about a quarter inch up the sides. When all the macaroons have been dipped, melt the remaining 4 ounces chocolate chips and scoop them into a plastic zipper bag. Gently squeeze all of the chocolate to one lower corner of the bag, then close the top of the bag, leaving a small gap so it's not completely sealed shut and air can escape. In the corner where you've pushed the melted chocolate, use scissors to snip a very small corner off the bag. You'll be able to squeeze a small, thin stream of chocolate through this hole.

Drizzle the tops of the macaroons with the chocolate, making a zigzag motion to decorate. Dry for several hours or overnight.

Thumbprint Cookies
(Makes 36 cookies)

2 ½ cups flour

¼ teaspoon baking soda

¼ teaspoon salt

1 cup (2 sticks) unsalted butter, at room temperature

¾ cup sugar

1 egg

1 teaspoon vanilla extract

½ cup strawberry jam

Confectioners' sugar for dusting

Whisk together flour, baking soda, and salt in a large bowl.

In a mixer bowl, combine the butter and sugar and beat on medium speed until light and fluffy, about 2 minutes.

Add egg and vanilla and beat until incorporated, about a minute. With the mixer on low, add the flour mixture and stir until just combined. Shape the dough into a disc, wrap in plastic, and chill for an hour (or up to a day).

Preheat oven to 350°F. Prepare 2 baking sheets, either by lining with parchment paper or by greasing and lightly coating with flour.

Roll the dough into 1-inch balls and arrange on baking sheets, leaving about 3 inches between cookies. Press your thumb into the center of each cookie to make an indentation. Fill indentations with jam, but don't overfill.

Bake about 15 minutes, switching the cookies between the upper and lower racks of the oven halfway through. Cool on baking sheets for 10 minutes before transferring to a rack to cool completely. Dust with confectioner's sugar.

Quick Shortbread Cookies

(Makes about 16 cookies)

1 cup (2 sticks) butter, softened
½ cup powdered sugar
2 cups all-purpose flour

Preheat oven to 350°F. Butter and lightly dust with flour two large baking sheets, or line with parchment paper.

In a large bowl, cream butter and sugar. Add flour and continue to mix until mixture forms a soft dough. Then use your fingers to gently form the dough into a ball.

Dust the counter or other surface with powdered sugar and roll your rolling pin in it. Then use the same surface to roll out the dough ¼-inch thick. Using a biscuit cutter, cut into rounds and place on prepared baking sheets.

Bake 16 minutes and check. Are cookies pale golden brown? If so, you're done. If not, bake a couple more minutes. Let cool on baking sheets a few minutes before transferring to wire rack.

Hannah's Lemon Cookies

(Makes about 36 cookies)

¾ cup sugar

1 tablespoon grated lemon zest

1 ¾ cup flour

¼ teaspoon salt

¼ teaspoon baking powder

12 tablespoons unsalted butter, cubed

2 tablespoons lemon juice

1 egg yolk

½ teaspoon vanilla

Use a food processor to whiz lemon zest and sugar till zest becomes damp, tiny, and mixed in, about 15 seconds. Add flour, salt, and baking powder and pulse to combine. Add butter cubes and pulse about 15 times—till the mixture looks like cornmeal.

In a separate container, mix lemon juice, egg yolk, and vanilla, then add to the mixture in the food processor and whiz about 10 seconds. Now you should have dough. If not, process the mixture a very few more seconds. Then turn dough out onto the counter and form into a log, roughly 10 inches long by 2 inches in diameter. Chill at least 2 hours.

Preheat oven to 375°F. When the dough is thoroughly chilled, slice it into ¼-inch rounds and place them on parchment-lined cookie sheets, 1 inch apart.

Bake 12 to 14 minutes. Cool on baking sheets for 5 minutes, then on wire rack.